Sand Dancers

Sand Dancers

Let the Dance Begin

Lynda Waterhouse

PICCADILLY PRESS • LONDON

*To Jenny Fell, my clever friend who knows the names
of wild flowers, the calls of birds, and who showed me
where Cassandra Marramgrass lives.
And thanks to Sara Byers who lent me her
shell sculpture for inspiration.*

First published in Great Britain in 2009
by Piccadilly Press Ltd,
5 Castle Road, London NW1 8PR
www.piccadillypress.co.uk

Text copyright © Lynda Waterhouse, 2009

A catalogue record for this book is available from the British Library

ISBN: 978 1 85340 982 0 (paperback)

1 3 5 7 9 10 8 6 4 2

Printed in theUK by CPI Bookmarque Ltd, Croydon, CR0 4RD
Cover design by Simon Davis
Cover illustration by Sue Hellard

Extract from *The Book of Faeries and Other Strange Creatures* by Nathaniel Relyveld, 1847:

The Sand Sprites

Little is known about these mysterious creatures apart from the fact that they live inside sand dunes and follow the rules set down in a book: *The Sands of Time*. They are winged creatures that have lost the ability to fly.

Male sand sprites are known as sand farers, and spend long periods of time travelling the deserts of the globe in sand galleons, or go to sea. Young males are known as surf boys. They spend their time learning the ways of the sea, preparing to be sand farers.

Female sand sprites either sift the sand to keep it pure, or those with the most talent for dancing become sand dancers. Sand dancers train for many a long year until they can perform the secret dune dances. Their feelings run deep and, when thwarted, they can bear a grudge.

Let us not forget the ancient belief that if they stop dancing then disaster will strike the earth.

Chapter One

'Hope is like a strong wind;
it can carry a grain of sand over thousands of miles.'
The Sands of Time

Cassandra Marramgrass sneaked away from her birthday tea party. She was feeling very grumpled and needed some time alone. Feeling grumpled was a strange mixture of sadness, happiness and crossness, and she always felt grumpled on her birthday. It was the day she missed her mother the most.

Cassie climbed out of the dune and crept as close to the beach as she dared. No one would miss her for a while. Her only guests were old Mrs Sandpiper, Lena Sealovage and her Aunt Euphorbia, and they were far too busy drinking endless cups of sage tea and gossiping to notice she'd slipped away.

It was a cold afternoon and the wind whirled around

3

her flowing pink dress, which had been a present from Aunt Euphorbia. The wind whipped up grains of salty damp sand which stuck to her face, but she didn't care – for the first time that day her unhappy feelings melted away. Her heart beat wildly as it pumped hot fiery thoughts around her body making her feel powerful and strong. She picked up a pebble and hurled it as far as she could towards a large rock, waiting for the thudding sound as it crashed into the sand.

'OUCH!' A small surf boy popped out from behind the rock, rubbing his head and looking cross.

'Rubus!' Cassie smiled as she ran towards her friend. 'Are you all right?'

The boy stopped rubbing his head and stood up straight. ''Course I am. Takes more than a tiny stone to hurt me.' He shook his wings and stretched out his skinny brown arms in a sand surfing pose and grinned at her. His skin was tanned by the sun and his loose, sandy hair was tangled by sea breezes.

Cassie sat down on the edge of the rock as she checked that no one else was around. Female sand sprites were not supposed to leave the safety of the dune and they certainly weren't supposed to talk to surf boys – not until they were old enough to be considered true sand farers, anyway.

But Rubus and Cassie had been friends since they were sand babies. Cassie could talk to Rubus about anything that was on her mind. Rubus always seemed to know exactly how Cassie felt, sometimes even before she knew it herself. They had both lost their parents in the Great Sandstorm seven years ago. But while it was known that Rubus's parents and Cassie's father had perished while helping others caught in the sandstorm, Cassie's mother had just vanished. Cassie knew that she was probably dead, but she badly needed to find out what had actually happened to her – and Rubus understood this more than anyone.

'Don't suppose you've brought me any snacks?' Rubus sniffed and scratched his chest, releasing the fresh tangy smell of seaweed. Cassie took out a large samphire bun and Rubus gobbled it down.

'Euphorbia always makes you a good birthday tea,' he mumbled between mouthfuls.

'She wouldn't approve of your terrible manners – talking and eating at the same time! You'd get a big frown for doing that.' Cassie pulled a face. Then she folded her long dress around her legs and stared out to sea. 'How is the sand surfing going?'

Rubus's sea-green eyes glistened. 'It's so much harder than sand boarding because you have to control the sail as well as the board. But I raced the other day and I came in fifth. There's a lot of work to be done, but I'm learning all the time. I'll take you out for a ride if you like.'

Cassie sighed. 'I'd love to, but I can't stay too long.'

Rubus swallowed the last crumb of samphire bun and wiped his mouth. 'That's a shame. I was hoping you'd give this a try.' He reached behind the rock and pulled out a long piece of smooth, shaped driftwood.

Cassie gasped. 'Is that for me?'

'All yours,' Rubus replied. 'Happy birthday!'

Cassie stared open-mouthed. 'My very own sand board!' she said eventually.

Rubus blushed. 'You've been wittering on about wanting one for long enough and I was sick of lending you mine. It's about time you had one of your own!'

Cassie jumped up and carefully hitched up her dress. 'Come on, Rubus. I'll show you!'

Rubus grabbed his own board and, giggling, they clambered to the nearest sand dune. Cassie glanced around to make sure no one was watching and then balanced herself carefully on the oval wood. Slowly, she shifted her weight forward and felt exhilaration flood through her as the board tilted downwards and began to slide, scuffing the sand and picking up speed all the way down, while Rubus weaved his board in and out of her path.

After about half an hour of running up and racing down the dunes, Cassie collapsed in a heap of giggles. 'That was such good fun. You knew I've always wanted my own board. Thank you, Rubus. I'll practise every day when I come home from school.'

Rubus smoothed the sand off his board. 'You certainly look less grumpled now. The look on your face earlier would have turned back the tide!' He pulled an exaggerated cross face.

Cassie stuck out her tongue and waggled her ears at

him. 'I can't help the way I look. Besides, it's against the Rules for a surf boy to speak so impolitely!'

Rubus's green eyes sparkled as he said, 'You must be breaking a few Rules at the moment.'

Cassie rolled her eyes. 'Rules schmooles! There are 623 Rules in *The Sands of Time* so I'm bound to break at least one every five minutes! From now on I am going to spend all my free time sand boarding.'

Rubus laughed. 'Are you sure you wouldn't rather be dancing? I hear the dance school over at Dreamy Dune is going to be opening again. And there are now only 622 Rules for you to break. Rule 623 has been repealed – it's no longer forbidden to dance in public.'

'Yes, the school reopening is all anyone's talking about,' Cassie replied. 'I wonder why it's happening now, after it's been closed for seven years.' She tugged at her hair. 'I know it is supposed to be every sand sprite's dream to be the prima dune dancer, but it's not mine. You have to be really special to be a sand dancer, and only the best become dune dancers. I'm not nearly good enough.'

'Sand dancers all think they're so special, anyway, so dune dancers must be really awful! I'm glad you don't want to be one.' Rubus pulled himself into a classic sand dancer pose and put on a squeaky voice. 'I am a sand dancer! Don't spoil my dress. I have to look beautiful at all times! My wings will only flutter and flap when I'm dancing!' He picked up a handful of seaweed and draped it over his head and shrieked. 'My hair . . . don't mess with my hair! It took me three days to get it just right.'

He collapsed on the sand and rolled around laughing.

Cassie mimed pumping up her arm muscles and put on a deep voice. 'And surf boys think that they are so cool, but they are so dumb!'

'That's not fair, Cassie,' Rubus said, his eyes flashing. 'We have to understand the flow of the tides and the science of the waves, as well as care about all the sea life. We also deliver messages because we are not the ones with the reputation for bearing grudges!'

'At least female sand sprites take things to heart – which is why we are good at bearing grudges. Sand dancers dress to blend in with the dunes, and when the dune dancers dance, they make the dunes sing,' Cassie retorted.

Rubus looked surprised. 'I never knew that it was the dancing that made the dunes sing.'

Cassie sighed. 'Why does everyone have to keep to their separate ways? There's so much we can learn from each other!'

'It's supposed to keep us safe.' Rubus peeped out at her from beneath his long fringe of sun-bleached hair.

'Surely you have to feel a bit of danger in order to appreciate being safe? It makes me mad! The only dance I'm good at performing is the Rage Stomp! And I feel one coming on right now!'

Rubus and Cassie stomped their feet, spun around and around, and chanted:

'Rat a tat rage
Rat a tap rage
Feelings surge
Like an angry wave.'

Cassie swirled around three times, swishing her hair around her head so that Rubus had to duck out of the way. They both stomped furiously and then flopped down, exhausted, on the beach.

Cassie looked at Rubus. 'Your dancing's getting better.'

'Just don't tell anyone. I don't care what we're meant or not meant to do, but I certainly don't want the other surf boys teasing me. Your stomp was great, though!'

Rubus chewed on a piece of sea grass and said in a soft voice, 'You could always try to get into the dance school. I thought you might want to join the dance school because . . .' He paused.

'Because of my mother,' Cassie finished. She took a long deep sigh. 'Marina Marramgrass was the finest prima dune dancer ever. Look at me. I am nothing like her. My hair is light – like bleached sand. My eyes are blue instead of green and my nose is flat and squidgy as if it has a barnacle on the end. Marina could twist and turn her body in the most amazing ways. My arms and legs are floppy and have a mind of their own. Everything about my mother was perfect. What is the point in even trying?' Cassie felt her toes beginning to itch into a rage stomp again and her eyes prickle with tears.

'If only she hadn't gone out that night when the sand-storm struck.' Cassie chewed her lip and her wings trembled. There was a faraway look in her eyes. 'I always wonder what happened to her. No one seems able to tell me.'

Rubus suddenly dropped the stick that he was digging with in the sand. 'Wouldn't the dance school be a good place to try to find out what happened that night? Didn't you say you once overheard your Aunt Euphorbia telling someone that your mother was heading there that evening? Sandringham Dance School reopening is the perfect opportunity. Didn't your mother love the place? You need to go there.'

Cassie's toes began to tap. 'Me, at dance school? That is such a ridiculous idea!'

'But you might find something out!' Rubus insisted.

'Like how hopeless I am at dancing,' Cassie replied. 'I'd never get in, anyway.'

As she watched the dark clouds knitting a frown across the sun, Cassie was reminded of her aunt's eye-brows. 'I'd better be getting back,' she said.

Rubus looked out to sea. 'Have you ever wondered what's out there beyond the sand dunes and the sea?' His face flickered with feeling, and it seemed to Cassie that his eyes changed colour in the way that a cloud passing over a rock pool changes it from green to grey.

'All the time,' Cassie said as she picked up her sand board and raced back towards Mite Cove.

Chapter Two

'Follow your heart, be good and kind,
and never pollute the sand.'
The Sands of Time

Cassie squeezed herself through a small peephole that led back inside Mite Cove. You were not supposed to leave the dune without permission – and you certainly weren't supposed to spend unsupervised time with surf boys.

Mite Cove was such a small, isolated place – a dune bug trip away from Silica City, with its vast network of dunes. All there was at Mite Cove was a sand factory where everyone worked sifting sand, a small square of shopping stalls and the honeycomb of kutches – as the holes hollowed out of the dune, where the sand sprites lived, were called. Cassie sighed. In a couple of years she would be expected to work in the factory; every female sprite needed to help restore and repair the dunes.

Cassie often used this peephole, situated in a deserted dune walkway, when she needed to escape – or to hide things. She slipped the sand board on to a ledge and then walked slowly back to the small kutch that she shared with her aunt. Rubbing some dune sand on her feet and arms to dampen the smell of fresh sea air that clung to her, she tiptoed inside.

Aunt Euphorbia was sitting by the fire snoring. Cassie felt a pang of guilt. All the dishes had been washed and the heavy shutters over the peephole had been closed, and that was really a two-sprite job. On the table was a slice of wild honey cake and a battered old box.

Cassie took a bite of the cake. All that sand boarding had made her hungry again.

She sat at the table munching and stared at the box. It looked too old and battered to be another birthday present. Was it meant for her? Surely there would be no harm in looking. She flicked open the box and peered inside. There, wrapped in a delicate gossamer fabric, was a pair of dancing shoes. Cassie carefully took them out. They were a deep red and made of very soft silk. The soles were worn and the silk was faded.

Euphorbia slowly opened her eyes. 'They were your mother's favourite pair,' she said. 'I thought you might like them. There are so few things left that belonged to her. Marina had such tiny feet.'

Cassie held one up. 'They'd almost fit me now.

Perhaps if I wore them I'd be good at dancing.'

Euphorbia's dark eyebrows knitted together in a big frown. She picked up her walking stick and banged it on the table. 'Dancing causes nothing but misery and heartbreak. Think yourself lucky that you are going to be one of the few Marramgrasses who does not go to dance school!'

Euphorbia joined Cassie at the table and she fixed her with her dark brown eyes. She reached out and brushed Cassie's hair from her face. Her hands were rough from doing too many shifts at the sand factory.

Cassie held the dancing shoes tighter. She liked the feeling of softness next to her skin. They smelled of roses and sea kelp with a hint of sea breezes – her mother's favourite perfume.

Euphorbia watched her carefully as she said, 'You know Sandringham Dance School will be holding auditions soon. It seems that everyone is full of the news and wants to give it a try. It's just as well you don't like dancing or I would have had to forbid you to go.'

Cassie sat silently, finishing her cake.

Euphorbia smiled. 'Despite what it says in *The Sands of Time*, being a sand dancer is not so special.' She took out a handkerchief and blew her nose. 'You are probably more like your father. He was a free spirit – and you're always sneaking off! He was always laughing and joking. He never took anything too seriously.'

'He was a great sand farer, though,' Cassie said.

'The finest. No one could control a sand galleon like he could. He said steering a ship was like wresting a jelly-fish with one hand tied behind your back.' Euphorbia chuckled. Then her expression changed. 'He was very brave during the Great Sandstorm. He rescued lots of sand sprites. When he heard Marina was missing he raced off straight into the eye of the storm.' Euphorbia's voice went quiet and she twisted her fingers in her lap before she swallowed and continued. 'I have not told you this before – it is not something I am proud of – but you are old enough now to understand how important it is for sand sprites to keep control of their feelings. Your mother and I quarrelled on the night of the sandstorm.'

Cassie felt her skin prickle. Her aunt had never spoken about the Night of the Great Sandstorm to her before, even though Cassie had asked her lots of times. She kept very still and quiet.

'I lived in Silica City then. You should have seen it before the sandstorm! It was a magnificent place full of large sandstone basilicas and palaces. My leg was aching really badly and that was always a sign that a storm was coming. I was on my way back from the late shift at the sand factory when I bumped into Marina. She was head-ing towards Sandringham Dance School. Your father was delayed so she asked me to look in on you until he returned. I told her I was sure a storm was coming but she was adamant that she had to go.' Euphorbia looked upset.

'Why do you think she insisted on going?' Cassie asked.

'I'm pretty sure that she was following an order. It must have been one that she dared not ignore – which probably meant it was from the Supreme Sand Sprite. When the Supreme Sand Sprite orders you to do something . . .'

'But why would she order Marina to go to the dance school with a storm coming?' Cassie's head was spinning with all this new information.

'Sandrine was a fine dune dancer in those days. She always spent a lot of time at the school. The gossips used to say that even though she was the Supreme Sand Sprite she would have loved to have taken the role as the prima dune dancer. But Marina was always just that bit better at dancing than she was. They were always fiercely competitive. They even had baby daughters at the same time!'

'Anagallis.' Cassie smiled to herself. She had heard many rumours about Sandrine's spoiled daughter. Then she gasped. 'We are known for bearing grudges. Perhaps Sandrine sent Marina because she was jealous!'

Euphorbia shook her head. 'Sandrine could be moody and temperamental but I don't think she was spiteful – although, of course, we can't be sure.'

The wind rattling the shutters startled them.

Euphorbia checked the shutters and said, 'Looks like there will be a storm tonight.'

Cassie stood up. 'I'll make you a pot of sage tea.'

Euphorbia smiled. 'My, you *are* growing up! You'll be

choosing to do your own washing and cleaning next.'

Cassie hugged her aunt. 'I'm not that grown-up yet!'

As her aunt turned to climb the ladder that led to their snug sleeping kutches, she said to Cassie, 'The best thing a sand sprite can do is to follow their heart, be good and kind and never pollute the sand.'

Cassie suddenly felt very determined.

'I will follow my heart,' she whispered to herself. 'I need to find out why my mother went out that night, and it seems that Rubus was right when he said the dance school would be a good place to start. Euphorbia thinks that Sandrine ordered my mother to go to the dance school. I need to know why. I am going to go to the auditions!'

Chapter Three

'When nature calls out to us,
we must dance in reply.'
The Sands of Time

Old Lena Sealovage was surrounded by a group of eager young sand sprites who were gathered around her market stall in Mite Cove the next day. They were hanging on her every word.

'I've just come back from Silica City. The auditions will take place at the next full moon, at the palace in the City. The repairs are not quite finished at Sandringham, and besides, it is very difficult to get to Dreamy Dune because it is so isolated. Candidates must be between eight and fourteen years old. They will be looking for sand sprites who can follow rules, work hard and, most importantly, who have natural dancing ability. A thorough knowledge of the seven basic steps of dune dancing also is a good start. And if you can throw your feelings into your dancing then you will definitely be in with a chance. Then again you may have all those qualities and still not get a place.'

'Why is that?' a young sand sprite asked.

Lena Sealovage tapped her nose. 'They are looking for that extra-special something that sets you apart. That elusive grain of sand that can make a true pearl.'

Cassie hung about at the other end of the shopping stalls and tried to look busy as she earwigged on the conversation. She did a quick calculation. The next full moon was in three weeks. That was not a lot of time to find out about the seven basic steps and to learn them.

'Are you buying or time-wasting?' Lena Sealovage grumbled at the crowd. 'Remember, it's buy one get one sea pasty free if you can say "She sells sea scones on the sea shore" three times, faster than me!' There was a scramble to say the tongue twister and buy pasties and soon there was only one left.

Cassie smiled and turned to leave the market but Lena saw her. 'Come over here, Cassie, I have something for you.' She reached underneath the stall and shoved a tatty book towards her. 'It is a few scraps of an old exercises book. It explains some of the basic dance steps.'

'Thank you, but I'm not at all interested in learning about dancing. I'm not going to the auditions,' Cassie told her. She didn't want her aunt finding out; she would only try and stop her.

Lena Sealovage winked and pointed. 'And this is not a sea pasty! You're a Marramgrass, aren't you? Despite what Euphorbia may say, sand dancing is in your blood! And after your disappearance yesterday, I know you do exactly what you want to, whatever your aunt may say. Take the book and think of it as a late birthday present. Please thank Euphorbia again for inviting me to your birthday tea party. No need to mention the book.' She winked again.

Cassie took the crumpled book. 'Thank you, Lena.'

Lena brushed her away. 'Now get out of my sight before I change my mind. Don't want people thinking I've gone soft in the head. I could get good money for that book. 'Then she leaned in closer and whispered in Cassie's ear, 'There is more than one way to peel a prawn, Cassandra Marramgrass. Time passes, sands shift and secrets are revealed.'

'I hope so,' Cassie whispered as she felt a tingle on the back of her neck. She longed to find out some secrets at the dance school. She slipped the book into her bag, and then quickly bought the few things that Euphorbia had sent her to the market for, and raced down to the beach in search of Rubus.

When she told him that she was going to go to the audition he grinned. 'So you've decided to take my advice for once!'

'Your suggestion did help, but I made my mind up when Euphorbia told me that she had seen Marina on the Night of the Great Sandstorm and that she got the distinct impression that she *had* to go out to the dance school that night – that she was following some kind of order.'

'Galloping sea spiders!' Rubus rubbed his chin. 'Maybe we're actually on to something!'

'So I need your help with this.' They found a smooth rock to sit against and Cassie showed him the battered exercises book.

'There are seven pages, one for each dance step. And there are lots of drawings of how to do each step,' Cassie said as Rubus leaned over her shoulder. She chewed her lip and continued. 'I've never really been taught to dance and there will be some sand sprites who know the steps really well!'

Rubus shook his head and tapped his ears as if he had water in them. 'That doesn't sound like the Cassie I know who wants to find out about her mother – the Cassie who is not afraid of anything!'

'I *am* afraid of sea slugs and of making a fool of myself,' Cassie said. 'But you're right – I *will* give this a try. I have to.'

'You can pick up most of these steps no problem,' Rubus said as he pointed to the pictures. 'You read out the words.'

Cassie turned to the first page. '*Step one – the Sand Stretch. A dancer must perform this step every day. You must always try to increase your stretch. It is important to stretch fully and to feel all emotions fully. A stretch must be followed by a plié.*'

And so they got up and stretched, trying to imitate the faded picture.

Cassie turned the page. '*Step two – the Sand Plié. A deep bending of the knees. Bending helps you control how you take off, how high and how fast you can jump and the speed of your turns. The slightest bend of the body can convey a feeling.*'

Rubus bent over, clutching his tummy. 'I am conveying to you how hungry I am.'

Cassie rolled her eyes. 'Be serious! I don't have time to waste.'

Rubus said, 'Seriously, bending is important for sand boarding too. All that sand boarding you've done with me will give you a good start. What comes next?'

Cassie continued. '*Step three – the Sunrise. Rising on the toes gives the dancer a light, floaty quality. It can also be used to give you strength. The rise and flow of the dancer's body is an essential part of dune dances.*'

And so they floated . . . Cassie thought she felt her spirits lift slightly as she practised.

'*Step four – the Dune Bug Jump. This can be performed in lots of different ways. Jump from two feet to two feet, from two feet to one foot, from one foot to two feet, from one foot to the other. The finest dancers can jump the highest.*'

'This is fun!' Rubus yelled as he and Cassie jumped up and down. 'I can jump higher than you!'

'But not on one leg. I'm the champion of that!' Cassie yelled back. 'You read the next one out.' Cassie held the book out.

Rubus took a step back and shook his head.

'Oh, I forgot – Rubus can't read!' Cassie joked.

A red-cheeked Rubus shouted back at her, 'I can read the direction of the wind. I can read the tides and the weather and the patterns of the stars. I can even read moods. I just can't read words!'

'No problem. I'll teach you one day, but only after you've taught me how to sand surf.' Cassie picked up the exercises book and read on. '*Step five – the Sand Glide. The dancer must never lose contact with the ground as she glides over it. Depending on the mood you can glide slowly or quickly.*'

'This is like sand boarding without a board.' Rubus slid down the edge of a small sand hill.

'Two more steps to go.' Cassie turned the page. 'Oh no! Some bits of this are missing. The edge of the page has been ripped. *Step six – the Dart and T—*. I can't read that bit. I can only make out part of the rest: *To dart is to move above the surface of the sand with legs stretched and toes pointed —*'

'We'll just have to fill in the gaps. How hard could that be! The Dart and . . . Top? Tip?' Rubus replied.

'Tap? It could be the Dart and Tap.' Cassie tapped her toes. 'Like before a Rage Stomp.'

'Why don't you ask your aunt? She knows a lot about everything,' Rubus suggested.

'She hates dancing and would forbid me from going to the auditions if she knew. I don't want her to get suspicious.'

'You sneaky sand sprite!' Rubus grinned.

'Only because I have to be. Now let's get on.' Cassie waved the book under his nose.

'So we have the Sand Stretch, the Sand Plié, the Sunrise, the Dune Bug Jump, the Sand Glide, the Dart and T-T-Tap. One more step to go! What is it?' Rubus asked.

Cassie screwed up her face and looked at the page. 'I'm not sure. This page is badly damaged too. *Step seven – the Dune Arabe— The dancer must stand on one leg while —.*' She sighed. 'It's no good – I can't make it out at all.'

Rubus stroked his chin. 'That is a bit trickier. There are so many things you can do whilst standing on one leg.'

'You could waggle the other leg,' Cassie suggested.

'Or waggle your arm, keeping your other leg bent.'

Together they tried out lots of different moves to fill in the gaps until Cassie flopped down on the sand.

'Thanks for helping me,' Cassie said to Rubus, who was now busy practising his sand boarding moves. 'I'll ask Lena Sealovage if she can help me with the missing instructions. And I'm sorry for teasing you about the reading. That sounded mean.'

'It's OK – you've promised to teach me, now!' Rubus said.

'I suppose I'm not really used to being friends with anyone my own age – apart from you,' admitted Cassie. There are no other sprites my age at Mite Cove and there's no time to get to know anyone at Silica School as I have to leave early to catch the dune bug back to Mite Cove. Not that sprites are queuing up to be friends with a Marramgrass these days! Oh, they say they are impressed by Marina's skills but some of the things they say when they think I'm not listening . . .' Cassie's voice trailed off.

'What do they say?' Rubus jumped off the board.

'They mainly whisper about how selfish my mother was to run off during the storm and how it's her fault that the dance school has been closed for so long. They say such a famous dancer should have stayed and helped out. I try to ignore it because Aunt Euphorbia hates it when I get into trouble for being rude or stomping at anyone!' A tear of frustration slid down her cheek, and Cassie quickly wiped it away. 'I won't let them get to me. I will prove them wrong when I find out the truth.'

'How are you going to get to Silica City in time for the audition?' Rubus asked. 'Didn't you say you had to be there by nine o'clock?'

'I'm going to sneak out and catch the early dune bug.'

'Those old beetles are a bit slow. Won't your aunt be suspicious too, if you leave the kutch so early?'

'I have to take the chance.' Cassie nibbled the edge of her fingernail.

'Why don't I give you a lift? The sand surfer can hold two sprites. I could drop you off on the edge of the city close to the palace.'

'Brilliant idea! It'll give me a chance to practise my driving!' Cassie looked over at the sand surfer.

Rubus groaned.

Over the next couple of weeks, Cassie grabbed every chance she could to go over the dance steps in secret. She got up early so she could read over the steps in the book before her aunt got up. She 'missed' the dune bug back from school so she could perfect the moves whilst she waited for the later bug. She sneaked out at night to dance on the beach. One time she narrowly missed bumping into her aunt coming back from the night shift at the sand factory and had to hurl herself against the side of a rock. She practised until her feet ached. It was only as she got up early on the morning of the auditions that she realised she never had asked Lena Sealovage about the missing instructions. But it was too late for that now.

Chapter Four

'A sand dancer should behave with decorum
at all times, remain in the background
and wait to be given her due.'
The Sands of Time

'Next!' the loud voice called out from the doorway. It echoed down the empty corridor to where the last four sand sprites were waiting on a hard wooden bench for their auditions. One of them got up and disappeared through the door. Cassie gripped the box she was holding tighter. Her heart was beating wildly. She had almost bumped into her aunt that morning as she was sneaking out. Then Rubus had been late. Fortunately there had been a strong sea breeze to carry them along but all the time Cassie had been afraid that she would miss the auditions. Here she was, though, finally. She had tied her hair back in preparation for the auditions and was trying to control her nerves.

'I can't believe that the dance school is reopening!'

gushed a voice beside her, interrupting her thoughts. Cassie turned to see a tall, thin sand sprite excitedly gripping the edges of her patched-up skirt.

'About time, if you ask me.' The third sand sprite rolled her eyes. She was smaller and dressed smartly. Her azure-blue eyes sparkled with mischief. 'Let's introduce ourselves,' she suggested as she stood and curtseyed. 'My name is Shell.'

The tall sand sprite smiled and bowed her head. 'I'm Alexsandra, but everyone calls me Lexie.' She looked quizzically at Shell. 'Shell is an unusual name for a sand sprite. Everyone I know is named after sand or the flowers that grow in dunes.'

'I am not like everyone else!' Shell beamed. 'I was rescued from a conch shell as a baby and sent to live here. I am now one of Sandrine's serving sprites.'

'At the palace? Wow!' Lexie said.

'I know – I'm lucky to live in a palace,' Shell agreed. 'For one thing, I didn't have to travel far to get here. I did have to do all my chores in record time, though. What about you?' she asked Cassie.

'I'm Cassandra, but everyone calls me Cassie.'

Lexie wrung her hands dramatically and sighed. 'Well, isn't it wonderful that we're all here? It has always been my dream to be a sand dancer.'

Shell ducked below Lexie's arms. 'Quit gushing, kid. Isn't there a Rule in *The Sands of Time* about that?'

The three sprites sat up straight and chanted, '*A sand*

dancer should behave with decorum at all times, remain in the background and wait to be given her due.'

'As if that ever got her anything!' Shell added.

They all burst out laughing and Cassie instantly felt less tense. The door of the audition room opened and a voice gave a loud, 'Shh!'. The girls struggled to suppress further laughter.

'What's taking so long? A one-eyed jellyfish could see that that girl who just went in can't dance. Likes fish cakes too much,' Shell hissed when the door had closed.

Lexie giggled but Cassie said, 'Body shape has nothing to do with it. It's all about interpretation of feelings. Isn't that the most important thing?'

She certainly hoped so. She swallowed and held the box containing her precious dancing slippers even tighter.

'You have to master the technique as well and that takes years of training,' Lexie added. 'My mother, Viola Seacouch, danced at the Harvest Moon Festival and was hoping to be become a dune dancer. Only the finest sand dancers were taught the secret dune dance routines. Then came the Night of the Great Sandstorm.'

Shell stomped her foot. 'Please don't go on about that! I'm so tired of hearing about it and how everyone has to work harder, be vigilant and never have any fun any more.'

'But things did get tougher after the devastation of the storm. A lot of sprites have struggled to make ends meet,' Lexie continued.

Shell's eyes flashed. 'When I get to the dance school I'm going to enjoy myself. Maybe hook up with a surf boy.'

'No way!' Lexie's eyes widened in horror. 'Surf boys are wild. They can ruin your reputation. I saw a surf boy once and he wasn't even wearing a shirt!'

Shell giggled. 'They might have something interesting to say. They get to travel all over the place.'

Cassie kept quiet about her friendship with Rubus. She knew that most female sand sprites were wary of surf boys – but that was only because they did not know any.

'Dance school would be a bit of freedom after being stuck at the palace, and I'm going to grab it if I get the chance,' Shell insisted.

'I just want to learn how to dance,' Lexie replied solemnly.

'What do *you* want?' Shell turned to Cassie.

'Answers,' Cassie said without thinking, and then she blushed. 'I mean, I want to learn how to do all the dance steps.'

'Me too.' Lexie grinned. 'Wouldn't it be wonderful if we all got into the dance school. My dream is to be chosen to perform the dune dances and become the prima dune dancer.'

'Dream on,' Shell laughed.

'Let's promise that if we get in we'll look out for each other,' Cassie said. She had always longed to have some friends of her own age. She beamed with happiness at the thought that these two sprites could be her friends.

The three girls stood up, held hands, formed a circle and squeezed hands three times. Then they took five steps anti-clockwise, spread their fingers wide and touched the person on the right with each finger, performing the Friendship Promise.

'Day and night,
Loyal and true
I will always believe the best of you
I'll share my time
I'll stick like glue
Never a flicker of doubt for you
I'll watch your back
I'll sift your sand
If you fall I'll take your hand
No question
No need for answers
With your friendship I'll take a chance
Do what's fun
Do what's right
Because
You're a true friend of this sand sprite.'

When they'd finished they all sat down together on the bench.

'This is a great chance for us,' Shell said. 'And now that we are friends, can I suggest that *when* we get into

Sandringham we don't keep harping on about the past. We won't talk about our past or where we come from or about our homes. Let's concentrate on each other and the future.'

Lexie nodded in agreement. 'No looking back!'

They both turned to Cassie. She thought about her Aunt Euphorbia and her life at Mite Cove and agreed, 'No looking back!' After all, she was only hoping to find out something new about her mother.

The door opened again and the voice boomed, 'NEXT!'

'Wish me luck!' Lexie stood up, and turned and waved before walking into the room.

'She's got grace and good muscle tone. Lexie will be offered a place,' Shell said confidently.

'You seem to know a lot about dancing for someone who claims they're only at the auditions because they want to escape the palace,' Cassie noted.

'At the palace I get a lot of time to study people. Besides, I can't help it if I'm naturally clever!' Shell's blue eyes twinkled with fun.

'Is the Supreme Sand Sprite Sandrine as scary as sprites say?' Cassie asked.

Shell laughed. 'She is impossible in the morning before her first cup of sage tea.'

'My Aunt Euphorbia's just the same. She can be grumpy for hours if it isn't brewed properly,' Cassie replied.

'What is it about sage tea?' Shell grinned. 'Even the

smell of it makes me gag. Sandrine will not make any important decision without drinking a cup.'

'I suppose she does have a lot of hard decisions to make, like stopping sprites from dancing in public – and making them work at repairing the dunes. There has been so much work to be done repairing Silica City. Ruling over the sand sprites these last seven years can't have been easy,' Cassie said, putting the box containing her dancing shoes on the bench. She began to stretch in the way that she had seen the others do before they went in for their audition.

'Being responsible for thousands of lives is incredibly tough. Sandrine has had to make some tough choices.' Shell looked serious for a moment, then stood up and began to stretch her legs too. 'I didn't expect to feel this nervous. I can't stop thinking that if I don't get in I'll be stuck at the palace for ever. There's so much I want to do and see. Things are changing. Once the dance school is open again then I'm certain other things will follow.'

'What have you heard?' said Cassie, finishing her warm-up exercises.

Shell looked at her. 'Nothing specific. I'm only a lowly servant. Nobody tells me anything.'

'What's Anagallis like? Do you ever get to see Sandrine's daughter?'

Shell laughed. 'All the time.'

'Is she as bad as people say?'

Shell groaned. 'Much, much worse.'

Cassie laughed. 'I'm glad. It is delicious to hear about someone who doesn't behave. People are always coming to my aunt with tales about me. "That girl threw a pebble at my window and pulled a face" or, "I heard Cassie burp twice and she didn't cover her mouth". Sometimes it feels like I can't do anything right!'

Shell took a deep breath. 'Both of us just have to get in, and I mean that in a totally non-gushing way.'

Cassie nodded. 'Our futures depend upon it.'

'This has come loose,' said Shell, pulling a strand of Cassie's hair. 'Let me do it. You want to look your best.'

They both sat down again and nobody spoke for a while. Cassie chewed the end of her fingernail and asked, 'What do you think they will be looking for in the audition?'

'Apart from the seven steps, you mean?' Shell asked.

'Sort of,' Cassie said.

'Earlier I saw them bringing in the shell head-dress,' Shell replied. 'So I guess we'll have to wear it and try to be inspired by the sounds we hear. They will be looking at how deeply you feel and how well you communicate those feelings.'

Cassie bit her lip. 'I hope I don't show myself up! I took a bit of a risk coming here. My aunt doesn't approve of dancing.'

'She doesn't know you're here? Did you sneak away too?'

'Yes,' Cassie said, nodding. 'You did as well?'

Shell grinned. 'I did! That's why I was late. Once I've been offered a place I'm hoping that Sandrine will let me go. It would be embarrassing if she didn't let someone who works at the palace have a place, don't you think?' Shell sat down beside her. 'It must be nearly your turn by now. They only seem to take a few turns of the small sand timer to make up their minds if you're out or you're in. I've got a good feeling about you, Cassie.'

'Nothing is certain,' Cassie murmured, wishing she had Shell's confidence.

Cassie's heart began to pulse loudly as the door of the audition room slowly began to open. She closed her eyes, taking a couple of deep breaths to prepare herself, when she heard the sound of footsteps as a voice boomed across the room.

'CASSANDRA MARRAMGRASS, WHAT DO YOU THINK YOU ARE DOING?!'

Chapter Five

'The wings of a sand sprite will only come alive
when she dances with all her heart.'
The Sands of Time

'NEXT!' The bossy voice from the audition room summoned Cassie as Aunt Euphorbia strode towards her.

'How many times do I have to tell you that dancing will only lead to heartbreak?'

'I'm sorry,' Cassie said softly.

'And you've taken your mother's dancing slippers!' Euphorbia's face was purple with fury.

'Yes, I did. I'm sorry.' Cassie felt that it was no time for any more lies.

'I see,' Euphorbia said as she slowly raised her hand.

'I am sorry. Truly I am.' Tears came into Cassie's eyes. 'I'm really sorry to be such a disappointment to you.'

'Is that what you think?' Euphorbia's voice cracked. 'Oh, Cassie.'

'Please let me at least audition!' Cassie pleaded.

'Excuse me.' A voice cut into their conversation and Cassie felt a sharp dig in her ribs. 'Do you mind if I go in front of you, only I have been waiting an awfully long time.' Shell performed the curtsey of respect.

Instinctively Euphorbia curtseyed in reply. That gave Shell the time to grab Cassie and push her towards the door of the audition room.

'Go on,' Shell hissed as she spun round on her heel and pretended to trip up, blocking Euphorbia's way and catapulting Cassie through the door.

The bossy voice belonged to a small, flushed sand sprite who prodded at Cassie and said, 'Hurry up. They don't like to be kept waiting.'

At the other end of the room was a table where two judges were sitting. One of them had a kind face and violet eyes. She smiled at Cassie. 'I am Madame Rosa Rugosa, the Principal of Sandringham Dance School. I want you to do your best and try not to be nervous.'

Cassie tried to smile back at her but found her face was frozen. She glanced at the other judge. She had six white braids that glistened on each side of her head. Cassie's heart thumped as she recognised her immediately. It was Sandrine, the Supreme Sand Sprite. It was said that her braids had turned pure white on the Night of the Great Sandstorm. Cassie felt her legs begin to wobble. She hadn't expected to find herself face to face with the Supreme Sand Sprite! Cassie immediately thought of Shell and the trouble she'd be in when Sandrine recognised her.

Sandrine pointed a long elegant finger at Cassie. 'Come along! Step forward. What is your name?'

Cassie bowed low and stretched her arm out as her aunt had taught her to do in front of royalty. She was aware of eyes watching her all the time.

'Cassandra,' she said.

'It has been a long day, and we have seen a lot of really good dancers, even more terrible ones and some that are an absolute disgrace!' Sandrine said crossly.

Madame Rosa continued. 'Tell me the names of the basic steps.'

Cassie nodded. 'The Sand Stretch, the Sand Plié, the Sunrise, the Dune Bug Jump, the Sand Glide, the Dart and T–T–Tap . . . '

Sandrine sighed impatiently and tapped her nails on the table.

'Surely you mean the Dart and Turn?' Madame Rosa corrected her.

'Oh yes, the Dart and Turn,' Cassie answered. 'And the seventh step is the Dune Arabe!'

'Dune *Arabesque*! Really if you can't be bothered to learn the names properly . . .' Sandrine tutted.

'I tried, but the exercises book that I had was ripped so I had to try and fill in the gaps as best I could,' Cassie explained. 'The instructions that I had only said *The dancer must stand on one leg while* . . . So I thought about all the things I could do with my body.' Cassie realised what a feeble excuse it sounded even as she said it. Every other sand sprite would have had someone they could ask.

'Put on your dance shoes and show us how you did that,' Madame Rosa said.

Cassie's hands shook as she tied on the slippers. She went through the seven steps, adding the bits that she and Rubus had created to fill in the missing gaps, imagining that she was back on the beach with Rubus and that they were dancing together. She went through each of the steps in turn, from the Sand Stretch to what she now knew was called the Dune Arabesque. She stood firmly on one leg and waggled her other arm and leg about.

Sandrine snorted as Cassie performed the step. 'Well, I must say I have never seen anything like that before!'

'It shows imagination and initiative,' Madame Rosa said. 'Now we have seen the seven basic steps – albeit interesting versions – it is time for the free interpretation using the shell head-dress.'

'I think I've seen enough free interpretation already,' Sandrine said sourly.

The little sand sprite handed Cassie the shell head-dress. It was heavy, made up of rows of tiny shells with two large shells that fitted around the ears.

'You have three minutes to respond to the sounds and

vibrations you can pick up from the head-dress. Do you have any questions?' Madame Rosa asked, her voice sounding muffled through the head-dress.

Cassie shook her head.

'Then begin,' Madame Rosa commanded, turning over a small sand timer on the table.

Cassie took a deep breath and concentrated.

At first, she couldn't hear anything apart from the beating of her heart as she moved into the centre of the room. And then slowly, first of all in her right ear and then her left, came sounds like whispers which created feelings in her . . . As the feelings came upon her she translated them into dance steps.

Her mother smiling and promising to teach her to dance.

The pain of her mother's disappearance during the Great Sandstorm.

Waiting, waiting endlessly waiting. The loss of her father, the brave sand farer, disappearing into the eye of the storm, sacrificing his life in order to save other sand sprites from the storm.

Her Aunt Euphorbia and their life together at Mite Cove.

Then her thoughts turned to the future.

To a possible future at the sand factory. Sifting and resifting sand for the rest of her life.

Back to the pain and darkness of being alone.

But the strongest feeling inside her was the need to find out what had happened to her mother.

Then a surprising feeling entered her body. Suddenly,

more important than anything else, was the desire to be a sand dancer.

To be the finest dancer. The one chosen above all others to perform the Triple Silica Jump!

To become the best dancer.

To be a force of nature.

To one day become the prima dune dancer!

Cassie felt her wings vibrate when Madame Rosa clapped her hands as the last grains of sand slipped from the timer. The small sand sprite helped Cassie take the head-dress off and signalled for her to sit down on a nearby stool.

Cassie bowed to the judges.

Madame Rosa looked up at her. 'You have potential.'

'There is something wild and strong-willed about her. Something Marramgrass!' Sandrine considered.

Cassie couldn't help herself. She replied proudly, 'That is because I am Cassandra Marramgrass, daughter of Marina.'

There was a stunned silence. Cassie couldn't believe what she'd done. There was no way that she would get to the dance school now! Sandrine, who had been jealous of her mother, who had sent her away . . . Why had she been so stupid?

Suddenly Sandrine banged her fist on the table. 'I knew it. From the moment you walked in there was something about you. Walk over there, turn round and spin.'

Cassie, confused, did as she was told.

Madame Rosa wrote something and then she looked up at her and said, 'Tell me, which Rule in *The Sands of Time* is the most important one to you?'

Cassie chewed her lip and said, 'There are so many Rules it's hard to decide.'

'Six hundred and twenty-two Rules to be exact,' Sandrine said.

'My favourite Rule is, *Honour and care for the dunes as a mother would for her child.*'

A smile softened Sandrine's expression. 'That is my favourite too,' she murmured. 'And which Rule do you find hardest to keep?'

'*A sand dancer should behave with decorum at all times, remain in the background and wait to be given her due,*' Cassie quickly answered.

Sandrine sighed. 'There are reasons for Rules, you know. Good reasons.'

Cassie felt her face go hot.

'The material is raw, but offer a place if you think you can make something of her,' Sandrine said with a wave of her hand.

Madame Rosa Rugosa said in a serious voice, 'Cassandra Marramgrass, you have been awarded a place at Sandringham Dance School. Term to commence by the next lunar quarter.'

Cassie bowed again and left the room by a different door, indicated by the small sand sprite. As it closed, she took off the dance slippers, exhausted – emotionally and physically. She could hardly take in the fact that she had a place at the dance school and a chance to find out about her mother. Surely Euphorbia would not be so cruel as to refuse to let her go. A smile slipped across her face. But then, even Euphorbia wouldn't be able to refuse an order from the Supreme Sand Sprite herself!

Chapter Six

'A sand sprite can never leave the past behind
– it clings like sand trapped between the toes.'
The Sands of Time

It was the evening before Cassie was due to leave for Sandringham Dance School. Cassie whirled her braids around. Sand dancers always wore their hair in braids, and that morning her aunt had taught her the special way the Marramgrass family did their braids, with an extra-tight twist and special arrangement of tiny shells.

Euphorbia had been very prickly with Cassie since the auditions. Whenever Cassie had tried to explain to her why she had gone, Euphorbia had raised her hand and refused to listen. Not that she would have told her the real reason – that she wanted to find out about her mother. That was a secret between herself and Rubus. But today, Euphorbia seemed resigned to her going.

Once they'd cleared away the remains of dinner, she handed Cassie a parcel saying, 'This is for you.'

Cassie was surprised. She had certainly not been expecting a gift.

'You had better see if it fits,' Euphorbia continued in a snippy tone.

Cassie opened the package and took out a dance practice dress. The fabric was so light that it almost slipped through her fingers. The bodice was a salmon pink and the skirt was carefully split into strips. Each strip was embroidered with dune flowers and grasses.

It was the most beautiful dress that Cassie had ever seen.

'I never expected anything like this,' Cassie gasped, slipping it on. 'It must have taken you hours to sew on all these tiny flowers and grasses.'

'I will not have anyone saying that I can't look after you.' Euphorbia's lips quivered as she spoke. 'The side panel needs taking in a bit.' She reached into her workbox, taking out a needle and thread, and instructed Cassie to stand still.

Cassie wriggled. 'There's no need. It's perfect already!' she insisted.

Euphorbia shook her head. 'The more perfect the practice outfit, the more perfect the dance steps will be. You have to look the part to *be* the part.'

'Then I shall be the most perfect dancer!' Cassie twirled around the table. 'One day, I might even be able to perform the most difficult dance step of all. The step that only the prima dune dancer can do – the Triple Silica Jump!'

'The Triple Silica Jump is the hardest dance step that you'll learn, but there is a simple secret to mastering it. You have to be fit and strong and flexible – that goes without saying – but once you are, it is simply a matter of taking three jumps, and making a turn of the hips as you take a very deep breath and *believe*!'

Cassie was amazed to hear Euphorbia speak so knowledgeably about dancing. As far as she knew, Euphorbia had never danced in her life, but it was typical of her to have an opinion on it – Euphorbia considered herself to be an expert at most things. But Cassie did not want to hurt her feelings so she nodded and repeated, 'Take three jumps, turn hips, deep breath, believe, and away I go!'

For a split second Euphorbia smiled and her eyes shone, making her look young again. Cassie smiled back. 'As soon as I'm strong enough I'll try it.'

Euphorbia finished the stitch and knotted the thread. 'You will not be strong enough for years! It is not going to be easy for you at Sandringham.' Euphorbia looked serious. 'It will be twice as hard for you because of who you are. Some people will expect you to be a great dancer and some will bear you a grudge. I know it is mean and unreasonable, but some sand sprites are angry with your mother for leaving during the sandstorm and hold her responsible for upsetting Sandrine so much that she closed down the dance school.'

Cassie smiled. 'I'll be OK. I know it will be hard work, but I'll have some friends.'

Cassie desperately hoped that Lexie and Shell had also won places. She had been thinking about them a lot lately. She pictured Lexie talking with her mother about what the school was like before it closed. She imagined Shell serving sage tea to Sandrine every morning. Cassie wondered how Sandrine had reacted when she saw one of her servants at the auditions. Maybe Sandrine hadn't even recognised her. But Cassie doubted that somehow, as there was a sparkle about Shell that was hard to ignore. She hoped that Lexie and Shell were at that very moment preparing to leave for Sandringham just like she was.

All the successful candidates had to meet at the Southside Dune stop of Silica City tomorrow. They would all travel to Dreamy Dune and the dance school together. This meant that she would have to leave Mite Cove before the sun rose to get there in time. It would be a long journey, but Cassie could hardly wait.

Euphorbia and Cassie sat by the fire until it was time to go to bed. Cassie knew she'd miss Euphorbia and she was certain her aunt would miss her – for all her severity, she never doubted how much she cared for her. But still, she was longing to be on her way. Cassie was so excited and nervous about going to Sandringham that she found it hard to get to sleep. What had she got herself into? She tossed and turned over all kinds of restless thoughts and feelings, before she found herself reliving what had happened to her on the Night of the Great Sandstorm again, becoming once more that little frightened sand sprite.

A rattling noise had woken her up. At first she thought it was her mother coming back. Before she had time to blink, the storm swirled around her. It felt as if the sand and wind were trying to break her down into small pieces so that she would end up no bigger than a grain of sand. She tried to shelter from it, but the force of the wind was too strong, and in the end she gave up.

Someone lifted her on to a sand galleon. She was too tired to even speak and she found herself all alone inside Silica City.

For days she wandered the pathways and the tunnels of the vast dune city calling out for her mother. Everyone was racing around trying to save their possessions or find their families or food. Cassie's tummy groaned with hunger and she had to try and grab what food she could. She spotted a large basket of food and instinctively grabbed a slice of sea aubergine. She was about to take a bite when it was tugged out of her hands and her face was slapped so hard that for a second she was too shocked to feel hungry.

She learned to wait until no one was looking and then grab the food and run away as quickly as she could, stuffing it into her mouth as she went.

One morning she was hanging around the makeshift market that had sprung up in the main city centre. She was hiding round a corner and watching a stall selling seaweed bread. As the line of customers grew even longer and the seller was distracted, Cassie ran and grabbed a slice and took off down a narrow track. As she raced along, she tripped on a stone on the track. She was stunned, but all she could think about was saving the piece of bread that had fallen from her mouth. She did not register the huge dune bug racing towards her. When she did notice, fear froze her legs, she closed her eyes and swallowed the slice. She did not want to die hungry.

The next sensation that she felt was a sharp claw-like object gripping the back of her neck and slowly lifting her up off the ground. Then a strong arm grabbed her and shook the dust off her as if she were an old dusty carpet. A damp handkerchief licked her face and a firm voice asked, 'Cassie! Is that you?'

Cassie blinked. She had been starting to forget who she was. The woman leaned on the walking stick that had dragged her to safety, peered into her face and exclaimed, 'Cassie, it is you!'

Cassie looked up at the face. It was just like her mother's – only much older and without the sparkle. It was her Aunt Euphorbia.

'I have been looking everywhere for you.'

Cassie was speechless. She started choking on the slice of seaweed bread. Once again Euphorbia shook her hard until the crumb was dislodged.

Euphorbia took Cassie to live at Mite Cove.

Cassie sat up straight in bed.

'I will never forget who I am!' she told herself before settling down once more and falling into a deep and peaceful sleep.

Cassie scanned the crowd of excited young sand sprites gathered at the dune bug stop the next morning where the dune bugs were slowly being loaded with baggage and eager young sprites. Eventually she spotted Lexie and felt hugely relieved. When Lexie looked up and saw Cassie she waved.

Euphorbia turned to Cassie and said in a sharp voice, 'I must be going or I will be late for my shift at the sand factory. Work hard.' She turned to go, then changed her mind and kissed a startled Cassie on the cheek, whispering, 'Don't forget: three jumps, turn of hips, deep breath and believe with all your heart that you can do it!' Cassie felt tears welling up in her eyes as she said farewell to her aunt, and went over to Lexie.

Lexie was also crying. She blew her nose hard. 'I feel so silly because I'm sad to leave, but I'm also crying because I'm so happy that I'm going.'

Cassie rolled her eyes and wished that Shell were there to make some funny comment about it all.

'Stop crying.' Cassie nudged her friend.

Lexie blew her nose. 'I'll try. How did your aunt hurt her leg?'

'I don't know. She's always walked with a cane,' Cassie replied.

'And you have never asked her about it?'

'My Aunt Euphorbia is not the sort of sprite you can just ask questions. She is too busy telling you things!'

'She does look a bit scary,' Lexie said, nodding. 'I think it's those dark eyebrows.'

'Let's hang on and keep an eye out for Shell,' Cassie suggested.

'It would be fun to have her company on the journey,' Lexie agreed.

'How did your audition go?' Cassie asked.

'I was so nervous, and Sandrine seemed tired and grumpy, but Madame Rosa told me that I had a good line, was graceful and had definite potential. I'm going to work so hard at Sandringham to prove her right. My mother says she is the wisest, most intuitive dancer in the western hemisphere.'

'Cassandra Marramgrass! Message for Cassandra Marramgrass!' A male voice cut across the chatter.

There was silence at the bug stop. Someone whispered, 'A Marramgrass? I hope not. They're nothing but trouble!'

Someone else laughed.

The voice continued calling out, 'Cassandra Marramgrass. Message for Cassandra Marramgrass!'

Cassie went cold on the inside as her face burned. She took a deep breath and walked up to the owner of the familiar voice.

Rubus smiled. 'I thought I'd better show up in case you wobbled like a jellyfish and changed your mind!' He bowed. 'Why do you look so embarrassed? I knew you wouldn't want to be seen talking to a surf boy, so I thought I'd make it look like I was delivering a message.'

Cassie scowled. 'Who said I was embarrassed? It's other people who have a problem with Marramgrasses.' Cassie pulled a face and said loudly. 'I AM CASSANDRA MARRAMGRASS!' Then her face softened as she shrugged her shoulders. 'I suppose you've done me a favour. No need to introduce myself as everyone now knows who I am! I was hoping to let the other sprites get to know me a little first, rather than avoiding me from the start because of what they've heard about my mother.'

'Oh, sorry,' Rubus said. He scanned the crowd. 'They do look like a stuck-up bunch!' He started to do his sand dancers' pose.

'DON'T do that here!' She pulled his arm down.

'You haven't even got there and you've already started to change!' Rubus shook his head sadly.

'I have not – but I don't want to get thrown out before I even get there and before I can find anything out about my mother.'

Rubus looked sheepish. 'Sorry, Cassie. You'd better get a seat on a bug. They are filling up fast.'

'I'll wait a bit longer to see if Shell turns up. I met her at the auditions – she's definitely not stuck-up.' Cassie scanned the crowd again.

Lexie came up to Cassie and Rubus winked at her. 'Is that a sea cake I see?' he asked, giving Lexie a bright smile as he bowed to her.

Lexie offered him one, saying, 'My mother makes them.' She looked down and shrieked. 'Is that your sand board?'

Rubus kneeled down and stroked the smooth piece of driftwood. 'This is my basic sand board and that is my sand surfer.' He pointed out a larger board with a sail that was lashed to a bush at the opposite end of the bug stop.

'That's so amazing,' Lexie gushed.

'With the right wind behind me I can really cover some ground. Ask Cassie. She has been on it.'

'You've been on a sand surfer?!' Lexie gasped.

'It's not that hard,' Cassie said. 'I'm sure we could make our own sand surfer if we wanted to.' She turned to Rubus and added, 'We'd probably beat you in a race too!'

Rubus grinned at her. 'One day, when the time is right and the winds are strong, we'll have to find out.'

Lexie added, 'And when we do, Cassie and I will tan your hide!'

Rubus smiled. 'We'll see! Now, I must be going. Good luck, Cassie!' Rubus strapped the sand board to his back and walked towards his sand surfer.

Cassie watched him leave before turning to Lexie. 'Where did "tan your hide" come from?'

Lexie blushed. 'I didn't want him to think he could beat us without a fight.'

They laughed and, linking arms, ran back towards the bugs.

'Shell must have taken an earlier bug,' Lexie said, looking round at the few sprites left climbing aboard the dune bugs. 'She's probably there already, getting herself the best kutch.'

Cassie nodded. Neither of them wanted to believe that she had failed the audition.

As they went to climb aboard the nearest bug, the sand dancer in charge of inspecting the permission slips looked them up and down. By the sour look on her face she didn't like what she saw. 'I am Calluna, senior sand dancer. I must say,' she turned to Cassie, 'I found your behaviour just now disgraceful! I suppose it is what we must expect from a Marramgrass. They seem to think they can come and go as they please.'

Cassie's toes began to itch with rage.

'Calluna's right!' another voice piped up, and others nodded in agreement.

'She was only receiving a message. It would have been rude to ignore him,' Lexie said, speaking up for her friend. Cassie smiled at her.

'It is far more important to maintain the honour and dignity of Sandringham,' Calluna said in a cutting voice. 'Madame Rosa shall hear of this.' She turned to Lexie and gave her a withering look. 'And that scruffy cloak you are wearing is a disgrace.'

The group of sand dancers onboard the bug giggled.

Lexie blushed. 'It's the only one I've got. My mother made it.'

'At least Lexie can wipe the dust from her cloak, but you are stuck with that nasty tongue!' Cassie stomped her foot.

There was a shocked silence. Calluna stood still, her eyes narrowed and her nostrils flared – like a sea anemone about to trap its prey.

'Come on, let's go and get another bug. Perhaps the company will be better!' Cassie took Lexie by the arm and they marched quickly away from stony-faced Calluna.

They had the last bug to Dreamy Dune to themselves. It was old and tired and seemed to take the longest way round to the school at the slowest pace.

'It helps if you put your feet in here.' Lexie pointed to the worn grooves in the bug's shell-like back as she stroked it. 'It's better for him. You know, I can't believe I've spoken to a surf boy. He was nothing like I imagined. He seemed to know you well.'

'Pretty much all my life,' Cassie replied.

'He has such green eyes, and what fun to go where you want and do exactly as you please. I would love to go sand surfing.' Lexie sighed.

'I can teach you. It's quite easy once you get going.'

'Oh, Cassie, that would be wonderful! And thank you again for sticking up for me. The way you answered

Calluna back was amazing. She is the most important student in the school – my mother told me. The senior sand dancer is like a head girl. She is given a lot of extra duties and responsibilities. She usually either becomes the prima dune dancer or a famous dance teacher.'

'Perhaps I should have shown a bit more respect – but so should she,' said Cassie frowning. 'She had no right to speak to us like that.' She looked fierce, then she sighed. 'I haven't even arrived at Sandringham and I'm making powerful enemies. Being a Marramgrass doesn't help. I suppose things could be worse. I could be Anagallis! No one has a good word to say about her either!'

'It doesn't matter to me who your family are. You are my friend. We swore an oath. I will always stick by you,' Lexie insisted.

'Thank you, Lexie. That means a lot to me.' Cassie felt a lump in her throat.

'As a Marramgrass you must know lots about dancing. Your family always produced the prima dune dancers,' Lexie continued.

'Not really. I live with my aunt and she has no time for dancing. Besides, I am nothing like my mother.'

'You are courageous and kind. My mother says that Marina Marramgrass was like that. She was always coming to the school to help train the sand dancers or to attend endless meetings in Madame Rosa's study. No one was allowed to disturb them, and they often went on talking late into the night.'

Cassie glowed. This was the first time she'd really heard anyone other than her aunt speak about her mother in a positive way. 'Did your mother go to any of these meetings?' she asked.

Lexie shook her head. 'No, she was only a student, and it was only the teachers who went, and Marina and sometimes Sandrine.'

Cassie begged Lexie for more details, but she couldn't tell her much more.

One day I will have to explore that study, Cassie thought to herself.

Then, changing the subject, she asked, 'I wonder how we'll spend each day at Sandringham?'

'Well, if it's anything like it was in my mum's day we'll have to wake at first light to dress and do our hair. Braids must be tied tightly and then pinned up. Then down for breakfast, followed by either a free interpretation class with shell music with Madame Rosa or a technique class with Mrs Sandskrit – apparently she is really strict. Then there are classes in etiquette and the Rules in *The Sands of Time* from Miss Youngsand Snr as well as sewing, mathematics, aerodynamics and geography with Miss Youngsand Jnr.'

'It sounds exhausting, but fun,' Cassie laughed. 'And did I hear right – there are two Miss Youngsands?'

'They are twins. Miss Youngsand Snr is the smallest but she likes everyone to know that she is the oldest so she insists on the senior and junior titles.'

All of a sudden the bug froze, then jolted them as it turned in another direction and began to make a low whining sound. Lexie and Cassie clung on tightly.

'It's calling out to another beetle,' said Lexie, shading her eyes with her hand and pointing to a silver speck on the horizon. The beetle began rumbling slowly in its direction.

Cassie spotted an arm waving and heard a voice calling out. 'YOOHOO!'

Chapter Seven

*'Always believe the best of your friends
– especially during hard times.'*
The Sands of Time

Shell was sitting beside a shiny silver beetle with a load of luggage strapped to its back. She screamed in delight when she saw them. 'I overloaded the poor bug,' she explained. 'These silver bugs are meant for speed and not haulage.'

Lexie gave the beetle a drink from her water bottle.

'All these bags have the palace mark on them,' Cassie noted as she helped Shell take off the luggage.

Shell laughed. 'These are the old bags that nobody uses any more. I'll just grab a few things and then can I hitch a lift with you? But before we do anything else – let's squeeze!' Shell opened her arms and they all stood in a circle and renewed the Friendship Promise.

'I just knew that you'd pass the audition,' Lexie said

when they'd finished and continued on with their journey.

Shell grinned. 'There was no way I was going to fail. I had to get away from the palace. I was getting so fed up of following Anagallis round and clearing up after her.'

'Didn't she want to come to Sandringham?' Cassie asked.

Shell laughed. 'Anagallis is as fat as a barrel and as boring as a barnacle – hanging around the palace whining all day. There is no way she could get a place at dance school.'

Lexie laughed. 'I've heard that too.'

Cassie squeezed Shell's hand. 'Thank you for distracting my aunt so that I could get into the audition,' Cassie whispered to her.

Shell winked back. 'My pleasure.'

'Did Sandrine recognise you at the audition?' Cassie asked.

'Of course she did . . .' Shell said. Then she quickly added, 'Actually I wasn't sure she would have done, seeing as I'm just a servant, but it turned out not to be a problem. Apparently, she didn't like the way I made her sage tea anyway!'

They talked and talked for the rest of the journey. Cassie and Lexie told Shell everything that had happened at the bug stop.

'A Marramgrass! *No way!*' Shell said. She thumped Cassie's shoulder. 'So you're Marina's daughter. Sandrine gets very grumpled whenever she hears that name.'

'I'm not ashamed of my name. I just don't like it when sprites make judgments about me based on it, that's all,' Cassie sighed.

'I for one am not going to be doing that. I've seen too much of it at the palace.' Shell smiled at Cassie and Lexie. 'You are my friends. That's all we need to know about each other. That Calluna sounds as mean as a sea spider! What does she look like?'

'She's tall — ' Cassie began.

'She's not that tall – I'd say she was about your height,' Lexie interrupted. 'But her expression is carved out of pure granite!'

'I don't think she'll be rushing to be friends with us,' Shell said.

They all nodded solemnly and looked serious until Shell asked, 'And what about this surf boy? Did he kiss anyone? I'm dying for some gossip. I've been so bored at the palace. Sandrine made me work twice as hard when I got back as a punishment for sneaking out to the auditions. I had to wash all the teacups in the Supreme Sand Sprite's Official Tea Service, and there are three hundred cups, not to mention the matching saucers.'

Lexie blushed and giggled. 'Rubus was charming. He bowed ever so politely when I gave him a sea cake.'

'There's no gossip, though. Rubus is not soppy! He doesn't go around kissing sand dancers!' Cassie said, defending her friend.

Shell laughed. 'I'm sorry. I'm just feeling so happy to be

free. It's making me say and do silly things.' She stood up on the dune bug, stretched out her arms and screamed. 'I'm FREE! WHEEE! FREE! Come on, join me!'

Lexie and Cassie stood up and they all yelled.

'Feels good, doesn't it?' Shell grinned.

It was almost dark when the three friends eventually arrived at Sandringham Dance School, on the edge of Dreamy Dune – the farthest dune of the group that made up Silica City. Like all dunes, from the outside you would not be able to guess the hidden worlds that lay beneath. The dune bug carried them down through the hidden doorway.

They jumped down off the bug, stretched their tired bodies, and took their first look at the school. It was a large, rambling sandstone building, and the huge mother-of-pearl gates at the entrance were closed.

'We're very late.' Lexie rattled the gate. 'I hope they'll let us in.'

'Doesn't look that grand.' Shell pulled on a bell rope that jangled and rang.

'Apart from the palace, it was the only building that survived the Great Sandstorm,' a gruff voice said, and an old sand farer came out of a small gatehouse and slowly opened the gates. He looked them up and down and nodded his head in greeting. 'I'm Thassalinus, retired sand farer and night sprite. Nothing gets past me, and I'm as rough as ropes!' He gave a throaty laugh. He took charge of the dune bug and opened the gates. 'You'd better hurry up!'

'It's finer than any palace to me,' Lexie said as she gave the bug a final pat and received a nuzzle of thanks in return. Then she turned to help Shell with her bags as they gathered their belongings and walked inside. They found themselves in a vast room with a high sandstone ceiling. In front of them was a large wooden staircase which led both upstairs and down. Lexie dropped the bags on to the stone floor and the noise seemed to echo through the building.

Calluna stepped into the entrance hall. 'So glad you could make it!' she said in a sarcastic voice. 'Punctuality is important here.' Her voice rang out in the vast space as she slowly looked them over, adding, 'As is cleanliness and neatness.'

'You must be Calluna. Thank you for such a warm welcome after our long journey.' Shell gave her a dazzling smile as she patted down her cloak, sending up clouds of dust.

Calluna wrinkled her nose and stepped away from them. 'You have twenty-two minutes until suppertime. As the senior sand dancer, it is my role to allocate rooms to my fellow students. I'll show you to them so you can tidy yourselves up before supper.'

The three girls smiled at each other as they followed Calluna along the corridor.

'The school is built on three levels. On this floor you

will find the dance studio, the dining hall and the class-rooms.' Calluna pointed at various doors along their way. 'On the floor below is Miss Youngsand Jnr's science laboratory, the teachers' rooms and Madame Rosa's study. No one is to enter the lower floor without permission. Our rooms are on the top floor. Each sand dancer has a kutch for sleeping in.'

They went up the large winding driftwood staircase and down a long corridor honeycombed with rows of snug sleeping kutches. They couldn't see anyone else, but they could hear chatter and excited laughter coming from behind many of the thick curtains that covered the entrances to the kutches.

'How many sand dancers are here?' Lexie asked.

'There are only twenty-five students who passed the auditions,' Calluna replied.

'There were hundreds when my mother came here,' Lexie said.

Calluna looked interested. 'Your mother was a dancer? What was her name?'

'Viola Seacouch.'

'Ah, yes. Seacouches are average dancers who are good for making up the numbers,' Calluna said as Lexie's face fell.

'There's nothing average about Lexie,' Shell said.

'Here is your room, Lexie,' Calluna said, ignoring Shell and pulling a small rope that opened a curtain. 'You are expected to keep your kutches tidy and be prompt to your classes and on time for your meals.'

Shell's room was next door. 'Do we get any help with unpacking?' she asked.

Calluna sneered. 'I'm getting tired of your jokes! Who do you think you are – Anagallis?'

Cassie was the last one to be shown to her room. 'Save me a place at supper,' she called out to her friends as she followed Calluna up a rickety stepladder and along a dark, narrow passage. The entrance to this room was covered with a piece of torn material.

Cassie looked inside. There was a small piece of polished mirror, a jug and bowl for washing, a trunk for her clothes and shoes and a narrow bed. It smelled damp and musty. From what she had seen so far it was clearly the worst room in the school.

She walked over to the peephole and opened it. To her surprise there was a small balcony with a rope ladder leading down to the beach. She tested the ladder. It was old but it would hold her weight if she ever felt the need to escape. She wished she'd been able to bring her sand board.

Cassie splashed some cold water on her face. It felt tight and scorched from the day's travelling, but she still couldn't help but feel excited. She had a place at the dancing school, two good friends and a chance to search for clues about her mother.

Something was happening in her life at last.

Chapter Eight

*'A sand dancer must always be the best she can be
in thought, word and deed.'*
The Sands of Time

After a quick wash, Cassie followed her nose to the dining hall. She walked into a large room that was buzzing with noise and filled with delicious smells. In the middle of the room were three long tables. All the other sand dancers were sitting at them. In the centre of each table was a large steaming soup bowl. Cassie's stomach growled with hunger as the aroma of sea vegetables and spices filled her nose. At the far end of the room was a large stained-glass window. In front of this window, on a raised platform, was another table, which was decorated with a fine cloth.

Cassie spotted Lexie at one end of one of the central tables and sat down beside her. All eyes were on the top table where the four teachers were sitting. Madame Rosa was sitting in one of the middle seats. She was wearing a pale pink dress with matching coral bracelets. She did not smile, but her violet eyes regarded everyone with a warm and friendly look.

Cassie was pleased to see her, and also relieved that Sandrine was not there. Her presence at the auditions had made her wonder if she was going to be closely involved with the school.

Cassie looked at the large sprite, wearing a bright orange dress, sitting next to Madame Rosa and immediately thought about Rubus's sand surfer with the wind billowing through its sails.

'That's Mrs Sandskrit,' Lexie whispered, following her eyes. 'Doesn't she look grand! She designs all her own outfits. She will be teaching us dance technique. I've heard there's no one better.'

'Who is the tiny sand sprite with the large glasses?' Cassie asked

'That's Miss Youngsand Snr. She knows every Rule in *The Sands of Time* off by heart, and that's her twin sister, Miss Youngsand Jnr. She has spent her entire life studying the science of sand dunes.' Lexie nodded towards a slightly larger copy of her sister who was moving from table to table with a large tray of laver bread.

'Here you are! I'm starving,' Shell said in a loud voice. She sat down opposite Cassie and started to help herself to some soup and bread.

There was a gasp from many sprites and Madame Rosa's calm voice rang out across the hall. 'It is more polite to wait until we are all ready.'

Shell froze, and slowly put her bowl back on the table. 'Please forgive me.'

Madame Rosa nodded. 'You are tired after your journey. That can be the only explanation for such rudeness.' She stood up to address the school and clapped her hands, making her bracelets jangle. 'Welcome, everyone, to Sandringham Dance School. Your dancing life begins today. It will not be an easy life. You will have to work harder than you have ever done before. Learning to dance is a pleasure, but it is also painful as each of you strives for perfection. A sand dancer must always be the best she can be in thought, word and deed. We are renowned throughout the natural world for our dancing, just as the sand farers are famed for their ability to travel over great distances. It is a great honour to be here. I hope each and every one of you is up to the challenge.' She scanned the room and it seemed as if her violet eyes met those of each sand sprite. Cassie felt the skin on the back of her neck prickle. Would she be able to follow in her mother's dance steps?

Miss Youngsand Snr spoke next. 'One of my responsibilities is to care for your health. You will all be given a bottle of special sea salts to bathe your feet in at the end of each day. I expect you to eat well, go to sleep early and look after yourselves. You cannot dance if you are not healthy. Anyone looking peaky will be given a spoonful of my famous tonic.' She held up a large bottle, which appeared to be filled with green slime. Everyone groaned.

Mrs Sandskrit then told them about the exercises book as she handed them out. 'Write your name in them and look after them well. There are spaces at the back for all your dance certificates and grades.'

Miss Youngsand Jnr peered out at them from behind her large spectacles as she spoke next. 'Each sand dancer will be given a sandbag to keep their sand slippers and exercises books in. In my sewing classes you will be able to personalise them.'

Finally Madame Rosa said, 'I think that is enough information for one night. Now, you may all begin your supper.'

The room began to buzz with chatter and the noise of soup being poured into bowls.

Cassie sighed and put her spoon down after a few mouthfuls. 'I'm too excited to eat much.'

'And I'm too embarrassed,' said Shell. 'What was I thinking of helping myself like that?'

With one swift move, Lexie swapped her now-empty bowl with Shell's. 'I can see that neither of you have ever had to fight for your share of food.'

'Looks like we're going to have to learn,' laughed Shell as they watched as Lexie slurp up all the soup.

As they walked along the corridor on the way back to

their kutches they they heard a noise and stopped. Hidden behind one of the sandstone pillars, a tiny sand sprite was huddled on the floor crying.

Instantly Lexie kneeled down on the floor next to the small sand dancer. 'Are you all right?'

Cassie joined her. 'What's your name?'

Shell added. 'And why are you snivelling?'

Lexie prodded Shell. 'Don't speak to her like that.'

Shell looked puzzled. 'I'm only trying to find out what's the matter.'

'Let Lexie try.' Cassie pulled Shell back.

The sand sprite wiped her eyes. 'I'm Gentianella. Everyone calls me Ella for short, and I'm really happy to be here, but every time I think about home I start to cry!'

Lexie smiled. 'You need to know about the Present Rule. My mother taught it to me. It's very useful at times like this.'

Ella wiped away a tear and looked up.

Lexie continued. 'You have to focus on being in the present. You have a place at the Sandringham Dance School. How exciting is that? Then you have to close your eyes and imagine that everyone at home is here with you sharing in your excitement.'

Ella closed her eyes and after a while wiped away a tear. 'I do feel a bit better.'

Lexie stood up and, reaching out a hand, helped Ella on to her feet. 'These are my friends Cassie and Shell. We'll look out for you.'

'But you're all so grown-up. I am only eight.' Ella frowned.

'Not so grown-up that we can't invite you to have a friendship squeeze.' Cassie opened her arms and they all hugged.

'Thank you,' Ella said. 'I feel so much better.'

Shell smiled. 'Now off you go and don't forget this.' She handed Ella her exercises book. 'You're going to need all the help you can get.'

Ella's face crumpled again as she began to wail. 'I'll never be able to remember all the steps.'

'Great job,' Cassie hissed to Shell.

'What did I do?' Shell said, bemused.

Lexie and Cassie both laughed.

'I hope your dancing is better than your social graces!' Cassie said, smiling.

Chapter Nine

'Never let your thoughts drift
in a sandstorm.'
The Sands of Time

When Cassie woke the next morning she smiled to herself
as she remembered where she was. Her first day at dance
school!

She got out of bed and stretched her arms and legs.
Then she washed and dressed carefully. Her fingers
trembled as she plaited her hair. In less than an hour she
would be taking part in her first dance class. Her tummy
began to wobble with nerves. Would she be good
enough? Would everyone else be much better than her?

She splashed cold water on her face and gave herself
a good talking to.

'Come on, Cassie. Stop worrying. Don't think too
much. You'll be fine,' she said as she gazed at her

expression in the mirror. She still looked a bit scared. She tried to smile, but that only made her look fierce.

The practice outfit fitted her perfectly. How clever Euphorbia was to make it without even measuring her, she thought. When she looked in the mirror again the dress had transformed her. It made her stand straight and she didn't look quite so afraid. She hoped her aunt was right when she'd said the more perfect the dress the more perfect the steps. She suddenly felt a lot better.

She walked over to the peephole, opened it and looked out at the view over Dreamy Dune and beyond. Despite her obvious intent to make her miserable, Calluna had done her a favour by allocating her this room. She could always escape down the rope ladder when she felt things were getting on top of her.

She smiled to herself as she made her way out of her room, down the stepladder and along the corridor to Shell's room.

She tugged on the curtain and popped her head through to see Shell still curled up in bed. 'Hurry up! You've got exactly six and a half minutes to be up and dressed and ready for breakfast.'

'Lexie told me I'd be late for breakfast too. I think she's already gone down. Let's skip eating and be early for class instead of late for breakfast.' Shell yawned. 'Your dress looks amazing. It's nearly as nice as mine. Would you pass it to me? It's hanging by the wall.'

When Cassie saw Shell's dress she let out a long

whistle. 'This looks like real gold thread.'

Shell slipped it on. 'Do you think it's too showy? Sandrine had them made for me because I was representing the palace.'

Cassie nodded. 'It'll certainly get you noticed.'

'Then I'll put something else on. I hate being the centre of attention.' Shell took out a simpler outfit from her trunk. 'I'll wear this one instead.'

They crept down the stairs and past the dining hall where Cassie tried to ignore the smell of crispy fried seaweed. They opened the large double doors that led to the dance studio. There was a lobby with long benches and hooks to hang your shoes on.

The dance studio was chilly and their footsteps echoed on the finely polished driftwood floor. The walls were covered in mirrors, but some of them were tarnished and the paint around the edges was peeling.

Shell poked her head inside and sniffed. 'It's not very grand. We have store cupboards at the palace that are finer than this!'

Cassie looked at the floor. 'We'd better put on our dancing slippers,' she said.

They both sat on a long bench and put on their slippers. As she stared down at the careful stitching Cassie's hands trembled. It wasn't just because it was cold. It suddenly hit her that her mother had once danced in this room and maybe even in these shoes. She quickly stood up and joined Shell, who preening herself in one of the many mirrors. Cassie poked out her tongue at her in the mirror.

'Call that a face?' Shell pulled down her eyelids and grimaced.

'Gross!' Cassie said, pretending to be shocked.

'There you are!' Lexie followed them into the room. 'I've been looking all over for you!'

'This room smells damp.' Shell sniffed as she put her arms around her shoulders.

'It's full of memories of other dancers,' said Lexie. 'They will guide us.'

Shell started doing a jerky dance. 'I can feel myself being controlled!'

Lexie and Cassie copied her as they moved around the room.

'I thought you must be here. I looked for you in the dining hall this morning.' Lexie sounded disappointed.

'We didn't feel like eating,' Shell answered.

'I ate a big breakfast and I slipped some sea spinach rolls in my pocket, if you want one. And I've brought something for Mrs Sandskrit.' Lexie placed a small package on the chair.

'Lexie, that's great.' Cassie took one of the spinach rolls and popped it whole into her mouth.

'Careful – they're still warm,' Lexie warned.

Cassie's cheeks bulged, and Shell pretended to be shocked. 'Now what would Calluna say if she saw that?'

They all giggled.

Lexie pulled her face into an expression just like Calluna's, and mimicked her sharp voice. 'I am shocked that you are eating in the dance studio. Whatever will you try next – dancing in the dining hall?'

They all shrieked with laughter.

'That is brilliant. Do it again!' Shell insisted.

Lexie did an even more over-the-top impersonation. She pulled a grotesque face and said, 'You have exactly thirty-three seconds to eat your breakfast, dress, dance and don't forget to burp!'

They were laughing so hard that they didn't notice the figure standing in the doorway until it was too late. Calluna walked purposefully across the room and placed some large diagrams around the room.

Lexie watched her in horror. 'We were only messing about. I'm really sorry.'

Calluna turned slowly towards Lexie and curtseyed. 'I do everything properly,' she said in a soft voice. 'And, Lexie, that includes bearing a grudge. Believe me, you will be sorry.'

Cassie reached out and squeezed Lexie's hand. It was cold and trembling. 'Oh Cassie,' Lexie gasped. 'I feel like I've swallowed an iceberg.'

Mrs Sandskrit sailed into the room at that moment, wearing a bright yellow practice outfit that shimmered around her large body like a heat haze in the sun.

She took one look at them and said crisply, 'You are early.'

Shell, Cassie and Lexie looked pleased but Mrs Sandskrit glared back at them. 'A sand dancer should arrive for her class exactly on time. Too early and she has probably skipped a meal and is trying to draw attention to herself. Too late and she shows me she is too greedy either for food or extra sleep. If you are to succeed, then absolute discipline is required in all aspects of your life. Is that clear?'

They all nodded, trying not to giggle.

'The correct response is "Yes, Madame". You will stay behind after class and assist the senior sand dancer with the tidying up. You might learn something from her about the correct way to conduct yourselves.'

'Yes, Madame.' There were no smiles this time.

The other sand sprites were coming into class and listening. When everyone was inside Mrs Sandskrit clapped her hands and the room fell silent.

'Welcome to your first day at Sandringham. You have all been selected for your potential. We are seeking to find those of you who have got the talent to make it as dune dancers. Here is where the hard work begins on that journey. We are going back to basics. During your first six weeks here you will be perfecting the seven basic dance moves. At the end of this time you will be tested, and if you are not good enough or if I decide that you do not have the right temperament, then you will be sent home. There is no point in keeping on sprites who are not suited to dancing. Is that clear?'

Everyone nodded. 'Yes, Madame.'

The words dried up in Cassie's mouth. She hoped she would be able to cope. She stroked one of the flowers on her practice outfit to calm herself.

Mrs Sandskrit paused and looked round at all the sand sprites. 'Let us not forget that your aim in coming here is to try to become dune dancers – the elite corps of sand dancers. Not all of you will succeed – some of you will fail. Most of you will make up the chorus, which is still an honour. Only the truly talented will go on to become the principal dune dancers, and from them the prima dune dancer will be selected. I wonder which of you that will be. The first steps begin today.

'Now let's begin with Step one – the Sand Stretch . . .'

Cassie took a deep breath and tried to concentrate. This was not how she'd imagined her first morning at dance school would be. If only she had ignored Shell and gone down to breakfast with the others . . .

She felt a hard tap on her shoulder and a flash of yellow in front of her eyes as she looked up to see Mrs Sandskrit standing next to her, staring at her with a fierce expression. 'You are not giving me your full attention. Look where you are now standing. You have drifted into another dancer's space and the line of your arm is terrible. Look at this everyone. Here is a perfect example of how *not* to do a Sand Stretch. The hands are all over the place and the feet are out of alignment.'

Cassie felt everyone's eyes on her and she would have run out of the door if she hadn't caught Calluna smirking at her.

I'll show you, she thought as she glared back at Calluna. *I am going to learn no matter how many mistakes or enemies I make!*

She took another deep breath and gracefully moved her arms into the correct position.

'Better,' Mrs Sandskrit said.

Mrs Sandskrit mopped her forehead as she called out, 'Bend and stretch, bend and stretch. Put some elasticity in your legs.'

She walked around the room correcting everyone's posture. 'A sand dancer must be able to bend as well as to stretch. A bend will give you the energy to take off and land.'

They had been working on combining Sand Stretches with Sand Pliés, and it was very hard work, but to her surprise Cassie found a deep determination inside her to keep going until she got the steps right. She bent her legs as low as she could.

Mrs Sandskrit came over to her.

'Feel the emotion as you stretch and bend. You will never be able to perform a dune dance without feelings. The ability to communicate your emotions is essential. When you are moving, think of the beautiful sand dunes and how they move and shift. How they are both light and strong at the same time.'

Cassie tried it again and this time she felt she was doing it better.

Mrs Sandskrit made them practise the moves over and over again, until the sand glass at the front of the room dropped its final grain.

As they were packing up she said, 'Before tomorrow's class I would like everyone to spend at least an hour rehearsing all the moves in your head. As well as lacking technical skill you all lack imagination. There is no fire in your bodies.' She sniffed and sat down for the first time on her chair, before jumping back up again with a loud scream. 'What is that?'

Lexie came forward. 'It is a sea pasty. I brought it for you as a mid-morning snack. I thought you would like it! My mother, Viola Seacouch, told me that you used to love your snacks, and I wanted to do something to please you.'

'Only hard work and excellent dancing pleases me!' Mrs Sandskrit snarled as she wiped the pasty off the back of her dress. 'Any more gestures like that and I will send you packing! Do you understand?'

A very pale Lexie nodded and whispered, 'Yes, Madame.'

It was only when they were removing their dancing slippers that Cassie realised how much her body was hurting.

'The Sand Dragon was giving you a pretty hard time.' Shell took off her slippers beside her.

Lexie gasped. 'Don't be so rude about Mrs Sandskrit!'

Shell frowned. 'I can't help it. When someone has made me stand for hours and twist my body into all these shapes it makes me say nasty things. I don't really mean it. It just makes me feel better. Oh no, look – my hair ribbons have torn.'

'I can mend them for you, no trouble,' Lexie offered.

'That would be great. I also have a tiny hole in the edge of my practice skirt,' Shell said.

'I can do that too,' Lexie said.

'I'm off for a swim. Do you want to come?' Shell asked after she had changed and handed over the slippers and practice outfit to Lexie.

'I'm going to flop in my room and study,' Cassie said.

'I'll join you,' Lexie replied. 'I don't think I could stand all the stares and comments about sea pasties.'

Up in Cassie's room Lexie rubbed some rosemary oil on to her legs. 'I can feel my muscles firming up already.'

'I don't think I'll ever be able to dance properly. My legs and my brain don't seem to be able to work together,' Cassie complained.

Lexie tugged at one of Cassie's braids. 'That's just it. You mustn't think about it! Dancing is about disciplining your body so that it can control the feelings and make them more beautiful and powerful.'

'It's going to be such a slog going over the same moves day after day trying to get them perfect,' Cassie grumbled.

Lexie stared out of the peephole. 'But when the dancing flows, everything changes inside of you. It's like that perfect moment when sunlight lands on the inside of a shell and makes everything that once was dull and drab look shiny and special. That's how I feel about it, anyway.'

'I hope that dancing will have that effect on me one day,' Cassie said but, as she thought about it, she realised that the more she danced, the more she enjoyed it. It seemed as if she'd been suppressing the urge to dance for all these years . . .

Lexie smiled softly. 'It will. I'm sure it will.'

Shell shouted up from the bottom of the stepladder. 'Where's Lexie? I need her help. The ribbon on my slippers keeps coming undone.'

'I'm up here,' Lexie called down to her.

'Catch,' Shell shouted as a pair of dancing slippers hurtled into the room, followed by Shell.

'I am falling apart,' she said to Lexie. 'I need your help.'

Lexie inspected Shell's shoes. 'I can repair these really easily.'

Shell flopped down on Cassie's bed.

Cassie sighed. It was beginning to annoy her the way that Shell expected everyone to do things for her. She looked at Lexie. 'You should show Shell how to do it herself.'

'I really don't mind,' Lexie said.

Shell grabbed the shoes back. 'You're right, Cassie,' said Shell. 'I really should be able to look after myself.' Then she rolled over and did a comedy fall off the bed, which made them all laugh.

'Wouldn't it be fantastic if we were able to become dune dancers and dance around the dunes of the world,' Cassie sighed.

'Don't get ahead of yourself. We have to pass all our dance tests first,' Lexie warned.

'The worst thing about the tests is that no one tells you in advance when they are going to happen. You just turn up for a class as usual and they test you. If you're not good enough then you get sent packing,' Shell complained.

'Don't depress us on the first day,' Cassie said, and she and Lexie threw their dance slippers at Shell.

Chapter Ten

*'Bearing a grudge is like walking on quicksand
– you are sucked under by the force of your feelings.'*
The Sands of Time

Time flew by as the sand dancers settled into an exhausting routine of dancing and studying. Cassie walked back into her room after supper a couple of weeks later ready to soak her tired feet, as she did every evening, when she sensed that someone was on the balcony. She picked up the washing jug and crept towards the peephole.

A gust of wind made the curtain billow as she reached out of the hole and prepared to strike.

Rubus jumped and screamed as Cassie groaned. 'Are you trying to ruin my reputation for ever?'

'I didn't mean to frighten you.'

She mimicked his startled reaction. '*I* didn't mean to frighten *you*.'

Rubus puffed out his chest. 'Surf boys do not know the meaning of fear.' He climbed through the peephole, backing into Cassie's practice outfit which was hanging on a hook, and jumped again. 'AARGH!'

Cassie clamped her hand over his mouth. 'How did you find my room?'

Rubus tapped his nose. 'Ways and means.'

'Thassalinus the gatekeeper told you,' Cassie guessed.

'How did you know?' Rubus looked guilty.

Cassie tapped her nose and said. 'I have my ways and means!' She wasn't going to tell him it was just a lucky guess.

'I had to bribe him with three bottles of sea shandy to let me in. He does tell the most fantastic stories about his days as a sand farer though. It's a really hard and dangerous life.'

'I should talk to Thassalinus. I bet he knew my father.' Cassie sighed.

'So how are things? It's been ages since I saw you. How are your friends?' Rubus asked as they climbed out on to the balcony, where he had left his rucksack. 'Made any others?'

'Not really – just Lexie and Shell. There's a young sand dancer called Ella who sometimes hangs around with us. Apart from Calluna, the senior sand dancer, everyone seems really nice.' She told him about the incident in the dance class on the first day.

He laughed. 'Sounds like she has no sense of

humour.' He reached into his rucksack and pulled out two boards.

'My sand board!' Cassie was delighted.

'I was passing Mite Cove and thought you might like it.' Rubus smiled shyly.

Cassie grabbed her sand board and they climbed down the rope ladder on to the beach. It was a clear evening with a pale half-moon. After making sure that no one was about, they raced down to the sea's edge on their sand boards.

'I'm glad you're having some fun,' Rubus said. 'Now have I got more chance at beating you at pebble-skimming or boarding?'

As they chatted away together, Cassie realised how much she'd missed Rubus and how easy it was to talk to him. 'I don't know how good I am at having friends,' she confided. 'It really bothers me that Shell lets Lexie run around after her. Lexie is forever fetching and carrying for Shell – or mending her dancing slippers!' Cassie complained.

'Maybe she's happy to do it because Shell's a good friend,' Rubus suggested.

'And if Shell was any kind of a friend she wouldn't exploit Lexie's good nature!' Cassie snapped back.

'If Shell's spent her life running around after Sandrine and Anagallis, maybe she's enjoying having someone running around after her. Are you sure you're not the teensiest bit jealous?' Rubus peered at her.

Cassie snorted. 'As if! I would not dream of letting anyone pick up my stuff or do things for me that I am quite capable of doing myself. No way!' Cassie swished her head so fiercely that Rubus had to duck out of the way of her braids.

'OK, I get your point,' said Rubus, raising his arms up to his face. 'How have you been getting on with your real reason for being here? Have you found anything out about Marina?'

Cassie looked a bit shamefaced. She had been putting off trying to find out about her mother because she had little idea of where to start, and the dance classes had exhausted her. 'I haven't done much. I've had to settle in and get on. They work you really hard. I've been letting the Marramgrass dust settle for a while so I can find my way around.'

'Tell me about the school,' Rubus demanded.

'It's much better than I expected. The classes are difficult, and Mrs Sandskrit is especially hard to please, but I think I am beginning to make some progress as a dancer. But I find it hard to be so precise with those seven steps. It is really difficult, and I'm trying my best, but sometimes it feels like that just isn't enough.'

Rubus shook his head and snapped off a twig from a piece of driftwood. 'What about the layout of the place – that's what I'm interested in.'

Cassie picked up the twig and began scratching the outline of the building in a patch of sand. 'The area that

I don't know much about is the lower floor, where the teachers live. Miss Youngsand Jnr's research laboratory is there, as well as Madame Rosa's study, but I haven't been into any of those places yet. I have found out that meetings used to be held in her study late at night so that will be my first place to look. We haven't started our science lessons yet, but I suppose I could go in there and pretend I'm looking for Miss Youngsand Jnr.'

Rubus stroked his chin. 'You should certainly try and have a look in there.'

'I'm guessing that all the dance school documents are kept in Madame Rosa's study. The only trouble is that no one is allowed inside without permission. Our kutches only have curtains but the rest of the rooms have driftwood doors with locks.'

Rubus let out a long sigh. 'A sand sprite I used to know would have said "Rules schmooles" and found a way to get inside.'

Cassie felt her cheeks burning. Rubus's words stung her. She had allowed herself to get carried away by the idea of learning to dance and becoming a sand dancer. Dancing was getting under her skin and making her forget why she'd come to the school.

Cassie nodded. 'By the next time you come I'll have taken a look inside that study. Now let's race. One good thing about all this dancing is that it has made me stronger. I bet I can beat you.'

'We'll see about that!' Rubus raced off on his board.

An hour later an exhausted Cassie climbed back up the rope ladder and fell into bed. Her body was tired but her mind was racing. It was focused on one thing: trying to think of a way to get into Madame Rosa's study.

Chapter Eleven

'There is a movement to capture every mood and emotion.
Dance and you will find it.'
The Sands of Time

As Mrs Sandskrit sailed into the practice room the next
morning, she announced, 'Madame Rosa has decided
that it is time for your first interpretation class.'

An excited whisper filled the room. Lexie, Cassie and
Shell grinned at each other. Mrs Sandskrit lifted up her
hand and continued. 'I am not convinced that you are
ready, but we shall see. Make your way in single file to
the swimming pool at once, and without any talking.'

Intrigued, the sand sprites walked as fast as they dared
out of the practice room and through the back corridor
that led to the outdoor swimming pool. The pool was
wedged between two sides of the dunes and was lined
with rocks and fringed by grasses and gorse bushes.

Miss Youngsand Snr was waiting for them by the swimming pool. Her tiny body was almost hidden by the row of gorse bushes by the side of the pool.

'Maybe we're going to do the class underwater.' Shell nudged Lexie.

'Shh,' Calluna said as she walked past them.

'Follow me.' Miss Youngsand Snr pointed to an old stone staircase behind a large bush.

'I've never noticed that before,' Cassie whispered to Lexie. 'This is exciting.'

'Careful on the stairs! They're old and slippery,' Miss Youngsand Snr warned as they all filed down. The stairs wound down and led to a small grotto.

'It's beautiful,' Lexie gasped. The walls were covered in shells and coloured glass that twinkled in the pale shafts of light. In the middle of the room there was a green shell fountain with a small white shell in the centre of it. Thassalinus was standing next to it.

'The perfect place for me.' Shell's eyes twinkled as she spun around, touching the smooth walls.

'Welcome to our outdoor dance studio,' Madame Rosa greeted them as they walked into the grotto. She was wearing a pearl-coloured dress and her arms were decorated with shell bracelets. 'It is time for your first interpretation class. A sand dancer should be always in touch with her feelings and sensitive to the emotions of those around her. This allows her to interpret these emotions in her dancing.'

The sand sprites gathered around excitedly.

Madame Rosa lifted her arms, making her bracelets shake. 'I will demonstrate a dance inspired by my love of the dunes to the accompaniment of the fountain.' She nodded to Thassalinus who began to turn the handle on the white shell.

The room fell silent as the water flowing through the shell made a gentle bubbling sound. Madame Rosa began to dance, slowly at first, and then building into a sequence of moves so light and delicate that even her wings began to flutter gracefully. It was the most beautiful dancing Cassie had ever seen. No one moved or spoke during the dance – everyone's eyes were fixed on Madame Rosa. Finally she stopped and there was a spontaneous round of applause. 'Now I want you all to have a go,' she said.

As the other sprites began to move, Cassie felt self-conscious. But then she began to focus on the sounds of the fountain, the trickling and splashing of the water, and her feelings began to take the lead. She found herself recalling once again the Night of the Great Sandstorm and the last time she saw her mother.

It had seemed just like any other night.

Her mother tucked her up warm and snug in her kutch. Marina stroked her hair and said, 'I have to go away.'

Her mother used to go away sometimes to perform dune dances, so Cassie was not too surprised.

'Are you going to do the Triple Silica Jump again?' she asked drowsily.

Marina sighed. 'I can't tell you where I'm going or for exactly how long, but I will be back by the next spring tide.'

Cassie yawned. 'That is a long time. Will you bring me back a present?'

Her mother always brought her the most wonderful presents from her travels: scarves and dresses and delicious-tasting sweets.

Marina laughed and gave her a big hug. 'I will bring you back the finest pair of dance slippers and then I will teach you some of the exercises that will turn you into the finest dancer that has ever been.'

'So that we can dance together?' Cassie asked.

'So we can dance together.' Her mother gave her another tight squeeze and said, 'Never forget who you are and what you can be!'

Cassie fell into a deep, happy sleep.

And then the storm came . . .

The next thing she was aware of was an arm gently around her shoulders and Madame Rosa's voice saying, 'It's all right, Cassie. Everything is all right.' She realised that she was shaking from the top of her head to the tips of her fluttering wings, and that everyone was staring at her.

'Sometimes, dancing has the power to awaken deep emotions and memories in us,' Madame Rosa said. Cassie slowly felt calmer and the other sprites turned back to their dancing. Madame Rosa looked at her gently. 'After you've eaten supper I want you to come to my study. There is something I'd like to show you.'

Cassie could not believe her luck. She was speechless. She was actually being invited into the principal's study – the room which she thought might well hold the key to her mother's disappearance.

Over supper Lexie said, 'That was amazing. I have never seen you dance like that before. But are you feeling all right, Cassie? You look drained.'

For a moment Cassie thought about telling her more about her mother, and confiding why she was really at the dance school – but then Shell arrived, and the moment had passed.

Shell put her plate down. 'Great performance this afternoon. Do you think Madame Rosa is about to offer you the role of prima dune dancer?' she teased.

'She's probably going to lecture me about showing off. No doubt there's a Rule about displaying too many feelings.' Cassie stood up. 'I'd better get going.'

'Good luck, and if you're leaving that soup, I can help you out!' Lexie was already slurping before Cassie had left the dining hall. As she went downstairs, she smiled to herself as she passed Miss Youngsand Jnr's science lab. This was something to tell Rubus! She tapped lightly on the door of Madame Rosa's study.

'Enter!' came the voice from the other side.

Madame Rosa sat behind a large, highly polished driftwood desk. She was writing.

'Forgive me, but I must finish writing in the Day Book. All events in the dance school must be recorded.' As Madame Rosa dipped her pen in a pot of squid ink and wrote, Cassie looked around. The study was smaller than she'd imagined it would be, but it shimmered and glowed with candlelight. The walls were mother-of-pearl, and Cassie noticed a strange narrow ledge running along the top of the wall. The small peephole had a large seat covered in different shades of abalone. Opposite the peephole was a shelf filled with exercises books and a large copy of *The Sands of Time*. On the shelf below it was a row of small hessian-backed books all labelled *Day Book*.

Madame Rosa finished writing, looked up and smiled at Cassie. 'How are you settling in at Sandringham?'

'I am finding learning the steps hard, but I am enjoying it,' Cassie replied.

'I have been impressed by your application and attitude to work. You have a rare talent for interpretation of feelings – a quality that is essential in a sand dancer. Watching you dance today reminded me of someone, and I want to show you something. Come along.'

She stood up and walked into the back of the study. Cassie followed her.

'Take a seat.'

Cassie sat on a chair by an old table, on which there

was a large lantern. Madame Rosa opened a small wooden box and took out some painted glass strips. She fitted them around the lantern, lit it and pulled long drapes across the window to make a screen.

'You might be surprised to know that your mother also struggled to master the steps at first,' she said.

'No!' Cassie gasped.

'Marina never gave up, and spent hours practising so that eventually she was able to perform the Triple Silica Jump. No one had ever performed it perfectly before.'

Cassie watched the lantern flicker and the image of her mother dancing floated across the room.

'I am showing you this because I do not want you to give up hope and lose heart in your own dancing. You must realise that dancing is very important – even more important than you already think. You have a raw talent, but that alone is not enough. You need to practise. This is not simply for selfish reasons; sand sprites need to dance to survive. There are those who say that if we stop dancing altogether and forget the secret dune dances, then disaster will strike.'

Cassie nodded. She was mesmerised by the sight of her mother's flickering image dancing on the fabric in front of her.

Madame Rosa sighed. 'She was beautiful. Look at the way she moves effortlessly from a Dart and Turn into a Dune Arabesque.'

A knock at the door broke the moment.

It was Calluna. She scowled when she saw Cassie. Then she curtseyed and said, 'Madame Rosa, you are wanted urgently. Mrs Sandskrit has asked you to come and look at one of the young sand dancers who has developed the shivers.'

'I'll be there in a moment.' Madame Rosa blew out the lantern and guided Cassie out of the door. She smiled and said, 'Never give up, Cassie.'

Cassie watched Calluna and Madame Rosa hurry down the corridor. In her haste Madame Rosa had not locked the door behind her. As quickly and as quietly as she could, Cassie went back into the room.

The air was smoky where the lantern had been blown out. She felt uncomfortable sneaking in after Madame Rosa had been so kind in showing her the slides of her mother.

'If I'm quick it won't seem so bad,' she said to herself as she looked around. She looked at Madame Rosa's desk but, apart from the Day Book, the pot of squid ink and a pen, there was nothing there.

'The Day Books!' Cassie's heart raced as she turned towards the bookshelf and peered along the rows of books. What was it Madame Rosa had said? *'All events in the dance school must be recorded.'* The books were crammed tightly together on the shelf. Sand dancers were methodical, so Cassie knew they must be in some kind of order. There was a space on the shelf for the current book, so the book beside it must be the one with the details of the Night of the Great Sandstorm in it, Cassie reasoned. After all, the dance school had been closed since then.

A sudden creak outside the door made her stop and try to still her heavy breathing, but luckily the footsteps passed by.

She took the Day Book off the shelf and began to skim-read through the pages. She was just about to turn over a page when she saw her mother's name and read about a dancing display she had given. Her eyes prickled with tears and her hand shook as she turned over more pages and read about the inspiring lessons Marina had taught, the talks she had given and the concern expressed about the health of the sand dancers. Hardly a day would go by without her involvement in the school. Cassie's throat itched with sadness, but at the same time her heart glowed with pride.

She realised she was getting distracted, and flicked through trying to find the pages relating to the Night of the Great Sandstorm. Towards the end she came to a new section with *Pertaining to the Night of the Sandstorm* written on a blank sheet.

Slowly and carefully she turned over the page. Her heart was beating with excitement. Might she find some answers at last? Instead she found a large gap where the pages had been neatly cut out. Cassie was filled with disappointment and confusion. Who would have cut out the pages? And where could she find them, if not here? But just then another sound in the corridor made her stop and freeze. She would be in huge trouble if she was caught snooping.

Reluctantly she closed the book and placed it carefully back on the shelf and, making sure no one was around, tiptoed out of the room.

Chapter Twelve

'Three steps forward and two steps back
is the way to make true progress.'
The Sands of Time

All Cassie could think about was those missing pages.
What secrets did they contain? What answers to her
many questions were lying in those pages about the
Night of the Great Sandstorm? Her head was so full of
questions she forgot to leap at the right moment in the
Dune Bug Jumps with Mrs Sandskrit the next day, and
landed badly on her leg. She darted when she should
have turned, and bent when she was supposed to stretch.
It was impossible for her to concentrate.

Over the next week she found she could think of little
else apart from the pages. She found it difficult to eat, and
Miss Youngsand Snr made her swallow three spoonfuls
of green slime tonic every morning to try and get her

appetite back. Shell and Lexie kept asking if she was all right, and were very worried about her. But Cassie didn't feel able to tell them what the matter was – somehow it felt that her secret was too big to burden them with.

She couldn't even get excited when Madame Rosa made an announcement one morning at breakfast. 'As you have generally been working hard I have decided that we will give a public performance at the Harvest Moon Festival in Silica City.'

There was an excited whisper around the room. Madame Rosa raised a hand for silence and continued. 'But before then it is time for your tests. And no, I will not tell you the exact time, but it will be soon. You have nothing to fear if you have been working hard and concentrating. After the tests I will select the most promising group of dancers to show our talents at the festival.'

Everyone in the room cheered, apart from Cassie, who was only half listening.

Cassie urgently needed to see Rubus. She knew she could talk things over with him and together they would work out what to do next. When she slept she would fall into a jumbled sleep where she was chasing her mother through a sandstorm. Every time Cassie got close, her mother would dance away or turn into a shimmering scarf.

Then, one night, she woke with a start, hearing the rope ladder creaking outside. Then there was a shadow at her peephole. 'Rubus, where have you been?' Cassie asked in delight. She felt so relieved to see him.

'The usual.' He grinned. 'Why are your lips green?'

'Seaweed tonic. Miss Youngsand thought I was looking peaky.' Cassie stuck her tongue out. 'But never mind about that – I have some news for you.'

She told him about the missing pages.

'The book wasn't damaged?' Rubus asked.

Cassie shook her head. 'No, the pages had been deliberately cut out. Why would someone do that? They must have something to hide.'

Rubus frowned. 'If it was that confidential they may have destroyed the pages.'

'It's more likely they've hidden them somewhere. Sand dancers do not like destroying things,' Cassie replied.

'We need to go back to the study and search for those missing pages. Come on. Let's climb down and creep round the outside.'

'What about Thassalinus?'

'I brought him some barnacle beer and sea pasties so he'd let me in. That should keep him occupied for most of the evening.' Rubus sighed as he looked wistfully towards the beach. 'This is a great night for racing. Still it won't take me long to get us into the study,' he bragged.

They crept slowly down to the lower floor. Cassie felt nervous as they moved quickly and silently along the corridor that led to the study.

Rubus rattled the mother-of-pearl handle as quietly as he could. Then he stood back, stroked his chin and sighed. He ran his hands down the wood, muttering something about looking for the weak point. Then he flexed his legs and cracked his fingers.

'What are you doing?' Cassie hissed.

'One kick in the right place and I'll have us inside in next to no time,' he said.

'And wake everybody up!'

'I can do a silent kick. I just need to prepare myself.' He closed his eyes, bent and stretched his legs and padded around slowly in a circle while Cassie patted her hair and took out a wire hairpin.

She put it into the lock and managed to open it in three waggles.

'Ahh! I was going to suggest that if my kick hadn't worked – though it would have done.' Rubus grinned as they tiptoed into the dark study.

'I'll look on Madame Rosa's desk,' Rubus said. 'You might have missed something before.'

Cassie went to the small window, pulling the heavy curtain back to give them some light, but there was no moon visible. She checked the window ledge, but its abalone surface was clear and smooth.

They searched as best they could, but there was no sign of the missing pages.

Cassie even climbed on Rubus's shoulders to take a peep at what was on the long shelf that curved around the top of the room.

'Can you see anything?' Rubus asked.

'Just move a few steps closer so I can reach my hand across.'

'If you'll stop digging your heels in my back,' Rubus pleaded as he stumbled. Cassie stretched forward. Rubus wobbled.

'I think I can see something.' Cassie extended herself further. 'It looks like a folder.' She pulled herself forward whilst Rubus tried to steady himself.

'I've nearly got it. Almost there!' Her fingertip made contact with the folder. In her excitement her foot squashed into Rubus's face, which made him lean and wobble some more, and in the dark his foot stumbled on the uneven floor surface.

'Got it!' Cassie picked up the folder, sending clouds of dust over Rubus, who sneezed loudly.

'Shh!' Cassie dug her knees into Rubus causing him to spin out of control. She let go of the folder, and it landed with a loud thud on the floor.

They froze, but only silence followed. Then Cassie began to lean forward. Rubus grabbed her around the waist as she slid down. Cassie's hand reached out, caught on the curtain and she landed with a bump on the window seat. She winced as she grazed herself on a small metal nail.

Rubus wiped his itchy nose and quickly bent down to retrieve the folder. Cassie slid off the shiny window seat catching her leg on one of the decorative studs, which made a snapping noise.

'These are just some pages from some old exercises book!' she said, holding the open folder up to the window.

'We'd better get going,' Rubus said in a twitchy voice. 'Uh-oh, I am going to sn— ATISHOOO!'

'Shh,' said Cassie crossly. She was so disappointed that they had not found the book or any clues about Marina. She picked up the tatty folder. 'We'd better put this back and try and tidy up.'

She climbed on Rubus's shoulders and edged it back on to the ledge.

'Maybe the pages did get destroyed,' Rubus said as Cassie turned to close the curtains.

'Or maybe we're not looking in the right place.' Cassie stared at the ledge by the peephole. The top of the window seat had clicked open, revealing a hidden hiding place. 'Look!' she exclaimed.

'You must have unlocked it when you landed on it,' Rubus said as they both stared in amazement.

'There *must* be something about my mother inside here!' Cassie put her hand in. 'It's too dark to see, but I can feel something. I think it's pages. I've got them!'

Just then they heard the sound of footsteps and Thassalinus's low, mumbling voice.

'We'd better go. We'll get into real trouble if he finds us. He's probably checking the doors and when he finds this one's open, he'll search the room,' Rubus warned.

'Can't we just take them?' Cassie looked longingly at the pages.

'Someone might notice they've gone before we have a chance to put them back,' Rubus said.

'But we'll have to sneak back in again anyway,' Cassie said, desperate not to put the pages back.

'That's just as risky – we could get caught with stolen property,' Rubus replied.

Cassie sighed. She looked down at one of the pages and read, *Sandrine is in charge of the situation and, despite our reservations, must be obeyed.*

As quickly and carefully as she could, Cassie put back the papers while Rubus opened the door carefully.

The sound of the footsteps came closer. It was too late! They were going to get caught.

'Who's there?' called Thassalinus.

Rubus quickly shut the study door behind him before replying, 'Aah! Here you are.'

'What are *you* doing here?' Thassalinus's whisper had a gruff edge.

'Looking for you! I forgot to ask if you wanted me to bring mollusc mead or barnacle beer next time.'

'A drop of mollusc mead always goes down a treat,' Thassalinus replied.

'I thought I saw a peephole flapping open down that corridor too. Do you want me to come with you? It might be dangerous,' Rubus said.

'Get away with you, laddie! I've wrestled with sea monsters! I'll soon sort out any danger around here!' Thassalinus set off down the corridor, grumbling.

Thank goodness for Rubus's quick thinking, thought Cassie, and quickly slipped out of the study. She took longer to lock the door as her fingers were trembling and her hairpin took longer to bend into the tight shape. Luckily, they managed to make their escape before Thassalinus returned and they sped as quickly as they could down to the beach.

'I'll be back this way in a few days' time. We'll finish the job then,' Rubus said.

'I don't know if I can wait that long.' Cassie tugged at a braid. 'I'm going to try and find a way to get back in the study and read those pages. When I held those missing pages I just knew that they contained something important.'

'We don't know for sure,' Rubus cautioned. 'They may not say anything.'

Cassie's eyes flashed. 'I just know they'll tell me something. I can feel it. The sand between my toes is tingling – that is always a sign.'

'I know I can't help with the reading, but you do need help with Thassalinus.' Rubus looked serious. 'I can distract him with some mollusc mead, which is twice as strong as barnacle beer. I can also get him to tell me some sand faring stories. That should buy you some more time.'

'I'll try to be patient,' Cassie said to herself, as she watched Rubus disappear on his sand surfer across the beach.

Chapter Thirteen

'The truth can hurt – that is why it hides
behind smiles and half-truths.'
The Sands of Time

Cassie felt she was so close and yet still so far from finding some answers as to why Marina came to Sandringham Dance School on the Night of the Great Sandstorm. She was sure that she would find some evidence to show that Sandrine had been jealous of her mother and had sent her out into the storm. She thought about creeping down to the study by herself, but it was too dangerous without Rubus. She couldn't risk being caught and sent home. Twice she decided to speak to Madame Rosa, but each time she stopped herself.

She wanted to confide in Lexie and Shell, but it never seemed to be the right moment. Besides, all they could think and talk about were the upcoming tests, or the routines they were going to make up for the Harvest Moon Festival auditions.

Cassie really wanted to improve her dancing technique, but it seemed that the harder she tried, the more her body refused to twist or bend itself into the right shape. She was desperate to pass the tests, but on top of everything else she was finding the Sand Glide really hard to get right.

'Your mind and body have to flow as one!' Mrs Sandskrit kept telling her. 'My advice to you all is to focus solely on your dancing. Nothing else must matter to you!'

Cassie tried to focus, but instead of studying she spent every evening staring out from the balcony waiting for a flash of Rubus's sand surfer. The days passed slowly.

'Come on, Cassie. You're going to be late for class,' Lexie whispered to her one morning at breakfast when Cassie's mind was far away.

'You look awful. I can lend you some of my elderflower gel to brighten the shadows under your eyes. Sandrine swears by it,' Shell added.

'Why should I want to try something that a spiteful, jealous person like Sandrine recommends?' Cassie snapped back.

A pink blush appeared on Shell's cheeks. After a long time she replied, 'She's not as bad as that.'

'That's not what I heard,' Cassie murmured.

'You really need something to help you remember the order of the Sand Glide, Cassie,' Lexie said. 'It might help if you put some elderflower gel on your feet!'

They all giggled at the thought.

'NO laughing and messing around during meal times, Alexsandra!' Calluna snapped. 'As a punishment you can polish all the tables after supper.'

'I was laughing as well.' Shell's eyes flashed at Calluna.

'Me too,' chimed Cassie.

'It's all right,' whispered Lexie. 'There's no need for us all to get into trouble. I can manage.'

Calluna stood up. 'Then you can all clean the tables.'

'Why is she so mean?' Cassie said as she watched Calluna walk out of the dining hall.

'She did catch me imitating her that time in the dance studio,' Lexie sighed.

Shell snorted. 'That's not the reason why she is especially mean to you.'

'What else have I done?' Lexie wailed.

'Something unforgivable,' Shell said. 'You are one of the best – if not *the* best – dancer here, Lexie. That is what she doesn't like.'

Lexie blushed. 'Am I? Do you really think so? I *have* been working hard lately.'

Cassie suddenly realised with a sinking feeling that Shell was right. Lexie was an amazing dancer, but she'd been so wrapped up in other things she'd never really noticed. She tried to push away the sting of regret that it wasn't her. Cassie realised again just how important dancing had become to her. She would never have believed she'd feel sad that someone was better at it than her!

'I am going to try harder for my mother's sake. Starting with my classes today,' Cassie told herself as they left the dining hall and walked towards the practice rooms.

At suppertime that evening, Ella came dashing over. 'Have you heard the rumour? Tomorrow is test day. If you are not good enough you will be sent home.'

'Oh no!' said Cassie. 'I've got to practise my Sand Glide. I'm hopeless at it! But there's hardly any time – we've got to polish the tables.'

Just then, Calluna came over and handed them dusters. 'When I return I want these tables to shine.'

'Am I the only one who can't do a Sand Glide?' Cassie said as she waved the duster. 'I can't stop myself lifting my feet up between moves. My movements are not polished. I don't flow.'

'Not polished, eh? I've just had the most brilliant idea for extra practice!' Shell announced. 'Put these on your feet and take a table each!' Shell, Lexie and Cassie wrapped the dusters around their feet and slid backwards and forwards along the long tables.

They were so busy gliding and trying not to giggle too loudly that they didn't notice Mrs Sandskrit pass by on her way from the kitchen having stocked up on sea pasties. She had to place a pasty in her mouth to stop her from laughing at the sight but reasoned that, as they were practising, there was no need to tell them off.

* * *

The next morning they joined the others making their way to the practice room where Madame Rosa and Mrs Sandskrit were waiting for them.

Mrs Sandskrit clapped her hands and everyone immediately fell silent.

'This morning, each of you will be asked to perform the seven basic steps of the dune dances. At this point in your training I am not expecting perfection, but I am looking to see who has applied themselves. You will be sent home if you have not mastered the steps to my satisfaction. So let the dancing begin!'

Half an hour later, when the sand dancers had performed each step as a class, Mrs Sandskrit clapped her hands and everyone sank down to the floor exhausted.

It had been so much harder than anyone expected. Mrs Sandskrit had made them perform the moves over and over again. They waited outside the practice room for their results.

'I was about as light as a loaf of laver bread instead of liquid and floaty,' Ella wailed. 'My feet and arms were all jumbled up during the Dune Arabesque and I could feel Mrs Sandskrit's eyes burning into me the whole time.'

'You tried your best, Ella.' Lexie put an arm around her.

'She seemed to look at me at the exact same moment I landed awkwardly,' Cassie groaned.

'The moves are so easy to do when there is no pressure, but the minute I knew that someone was looking at me, my legs went all wobbly,' Shell grumbled.

'If you can't perform under pressure then you will never make it as a sand dancer,' Calluna said, coming up beside them.

'It's easier for those who don't have any feelings in the first place,' Shell hissed back at her.

Calluna blushed, and kept walking.

'That was uncalled for, Shell,' Lexie said, when Calluna had gone.

'But she picks on you all the time. She deserves all she gets,' Shell replied.

'I don't think we need to stoop to her level to beat her, that's all,' Lexie commented.

Mrs Sandskrit appeared at the door to call them back into the room.

'The hard work is beginning to pay off,' she said to them all. 'I am seeing some glimmers of commitment and discipline.'

There was a big sigh of relief around the room. Lexie squeezed Cassie's hand and Shell winked at her friends.

Then Madame Rosa spoke. 'There are some sand sprites who are performing well below their best. I am not going to send anybody home, but there is no room at Sandringham for dancers who cannot give everything.'

Cassie could barely believe it; she had passed the tests. She swallowed hard to stop the tears from coming.

Chapter Fourteen

'Dance, dance on the edge of the dune,
by the light of a large and kind harvest moon.'
The Sands of Time

In the dining hall the next day Mrs Sandskrit clapped her hands for quiet. 'Tomorrow the eight best sand dancers will be chosen for the dancing display at the Harvest Moon Festival. You have until then to perfect your dance routines.'

There was an excited flutter around the room.

Madame Rosa smiled and added, 'Those of you who do not get picked will be allowed to come along to Silica City to support the others.'

There was a loud cheer. The Harvest Moon Festival was lots of fun, with all kinds of celebrations, games and cake stalls.

'Be warned! I have a special medicine for sand

dancers who eat too much cake!' Miss Youngsand Snr said, taking out a large bottle filled with purple liquid from her pocket.

'Your families are, of course, welcome to attend,' Miss Youngsand Jnr continued.

Madame Rosa stopped smiling and looked serious. 'This will be a good experience, as it will help us decide who should be picked as the principal dancers for learning the dune dances next term. The prima dune dancer will probably come from one of this group.'

Cassie's heart beat faster. She thought about her mother, the last prima dune dancer, and suddenly it mattered more than anything to be picked. She knew her dancing had not been so good lately, but if she concentrated and tried really hard she might just scrape a place. She had to be one of the dancers! That meant she had to push down all thoughts of the missing pages and finding out what happened to her mother.

'Now eat up your breakfast and we will see you in the practice room in one hour!' Mrs Sandskrit said.

As they were clearing away their plates, Shell came over to Cassie. 'Lexie is going to help me go over the dance steps. Do you want to come?'

Cassie shook her head. 'I just want to go over the steps in my head.' She needed some time alone to try and focus her mind.

'To your places!' Mrs Sandskrit commanded as the

auditions began the next day in the practice room. Madame Rosa sat at a table and watched everything they did.

'It feels like the entrance auditions all over again,' Lexie whispered as they moved to their starting positions.

'At least we don't have Sandrine staring down at us,' said Cassie. 'When I saw her there my heart sank.'

'I thought she'd always be coming to Sandringham to check up on us,' Lexie added.

'Thank goodness she hasn't,' Cassie muttered.

'Sandrine is not that bad,' Shell said.

Cassie laughed. 'You have changed your tune. When we met you were full of complaints about Sandrine and how miserable you were at the palace.'

'Now that I have a bit of distance from Sandrine and the palace, I can see that you do need discipline and structure to help you be the best you can,' Shell sighed.

The audition began and Cassie struggled to keep up. Unlike in the test, when they had had to show how they had mastered the steps separately, here they were integrating the steps into dance routines. Each of them had been working on individual dances over the weeks, and they had the chance to display these, too. Cassie caught Mrs Sandskrit looking at her a few times and she tried even harder.

At the end everyone waited to find out who had been selected, but Mrs Sandskrit simply said, 'I need some time to consult with Madame Rosa. We will let you know our decision after supper.'

'Come on, let's go for a swim,' Cassie suggested to Ella. 'We're all wound up after the audition. We need to do something to take our minds off it.'

'I don't think my character can stand up to being tested much more,' Ella said and everyone laughed as they ran down to the pool.

Splashing about in the water did help them relax.

Shell rubbed her hair with a towel. 'My braids are all soggy.'

'I'll re-do them for you,' Lexie offered.

Shell shook her head. 'I think I can manage. I've been practising. It's about time I did things for myself.'

There was a nervous buzz at supper that night. 'Please let me have done enough to be picked,' Cassie whispered to herself as Madame Rosa stood up to announce who had been chosen. She desperately wanted to dance at the Harvest Moon Festival. She could hardly breathe as she waited for Madame Rosa to read out the names.

Lexie's name was one of the first, along with Calluna's and Shell's. There was a ripple of surprise around the room when Ella's name was called out.

Cassie carried on listening out for her name for a long time after Madame Rosa had finished, but gradually realisation dawned on her. She had not been chosen.

'There must be some mistake,' she said to herself. 'I thought I would just scrape a place.'

Shell gave her arm a sympathetic squeeze. She looked hurt when Cassie pulled away.

'What about Cassie?' Ella asked.

Lexie said, 'They've missed you out! They must have forgotten to call out your name.'

All the colour drained from Cassie's face. 'I just wasn't good enough,' she said sadly.

Cassie kept a brave face until she got to her room. Then she fell on her bed and sobbed and sobbed.

She didn't hear the knock but felt a hand on her shoulder. She was about to shrug it off when a voice said, 'Drink this.' Madame Rosa handed her a cool drink.

Cassie sat up and wiped away her tears as Madame Rosa asked, 'Why are you crying? Is it just a tantrum because you haven't been picked?'

'No!' Cassie wiped away her tears. 'I wasn't picked because I wasn't good enough. But I know I can be. Truly I know I can be . . .'

'So what are you going to do about it?' Madame Rosa looked serious.

Cassie stood up. 'First of all I'm going to go on to the beach and perform a Rage Stomp. That will make me feel better. And then I am going to grit my teeth and practise and practise! I will show everyone that I *am* good enough to be a dune dancer.'

Madame Rosa smiled. 'That's the Marramgrass spirit! When it comes to passion and expression in your dancing, you are one of the best. That is a talent that cannot be taught. But a sand dancer needs to be technically excellent as well. That only comes with practice – and you seem to have been distracted recently.'

Cassie's eyes met Madame Rosa's. 'There have been some important things on my mind, but nothing matters more to me than to become the best sand dancer that I can be. I want my mother to have been proud of me.'

It was really hard for Cassie to watch her friends rehearse for the Harvest Moon Festival. They tried to include her, but she often felt left out when they went for extra lessons or had conversations after supper about the dance routine or what their costumes were going to be like.

She kept watching out for opportunities to return to Madame Rosa's study, but it was not easy. Madame Rosa worked very hard and, when she was not taking classes, she was always in her study – and once when Cassie sneaked down, she discovered a late meeting was taking place, and she was lucky not to be caught.

Cassie spent a lot of time going over the basic dance moves. When she wasn't practising them she would draw the moves into the sand and then try to work out the best way to perform them properly. She decided that she would show everyone – one day she would perform the Triple Silica Jump and prove herself! For the first time in a while Cassie thought about her Aunt

Euphorbia. Of course, she had written to her and had letters from her, but she was longing to see her too. Cassie hoped she was well and not working too hard at the sand factory. What was the advice she had given her for performing a Triple Silica Jump? Cassie tried to remember. *It is simply a matter of taking three jumps, and making a turn of the hips as you take a very deep breath and believe!* It helped take her mind off things. It was hard at first to put all the instructions together. Sometimes she felt confident, but her hips would not twist at the right point no matter how hard she tried.

She did not just try to be a model student in her dance lessons. She really paid attention in mathematics and aerodynamics. She even listened very carefully to Miss Youngsand Jnr's long lectures about the science of dunes.

Calluna had made a point of coming over to Cassie after one of those lessons and saying in a superior voice, 'We are having special dresses made for the festival and we can sew shells and ribbons on to our dance slippers to make them unique.'

Cassie took a deep breath. 'That sounds wonderful. I hope it all goes well. You deserve your place as you have worked hard. It can't be easy keeping us all under control.'

Calluna looked taken aback. The hard look in her eyes softened ever so slightly.

'No, it's not. It is a very responsible job being the

senior sand dancer. I can't let the dance school down, or my family. My mother expects me to be the best. It's like having a big sandbag on my shoulders all the time.'

For the first time Cassie thought that there was a reason why Calluna felt she had to be so mean all the time. It also made her think about her own mother. What would Marina expect of her?

Chapter Fifteen

*'Two wrongs can sometimes make
the right thing happen.'*
The Sands of Time

One night Cassie waited on the balcony for Rubus. Madame Rosa had told them the previous week that she was going to be away for a couple of days, and Cassie knew she had to take this opportunity to read what was on those missing pages. However, the more she thought about it, the more she realised that it would be safer to have someone on look-out for her – and that someone had to be Rubus. But Rubus was taking an age coming back. In desperation, she had begged Thassalinus to try to contact him, and the old gatekeeper told her that she could expect him that evening.

It had been a long and emotional day, and soon Cassie's eyelids were heavy and she found herself asleep.

Her dreams took her back to Madame Rosa's study. Once again she was watching the images of her mother as she stretched her arms and crossed her feet, once, twice and again into the Triple Silica Jump. Cassie could almost feel her mother close to her, twirling, swirling, leaping and turning in the flickering light. It seemed that the light was following her. She woke with a start. Even with her eyes open she still saw the light. She closed her eyes tight and opened them again.

'Cassie?' a voice called.

Through her half-opened eyes she saw Rubus. In each hand he held a small glass jar that gave off a green glow.

'Glow-bug jars!' He held one out to her. 'I thought they'd help you to see better in the study.'

'That's a great idea. So much better than the last idea you had about kicking down Madame Rosa's door!' she joked as they crept down the rope ladder and made their way along the outside of the school towards the main gate. When she teased Rubus she felt less scared.

Rubus pointed to a small leather pouch attached to his waist. 'I've brought a large flask of mollusc mead. A few drops of this should loosen Thassalinus's tongue. I may not be a reader, but I'm a very good listener!'

Cassie hid behind a rock as Rubus called out to the night sprite. He was so distracted with the fuss Rubus made of him and with the mead that Cassie easily slipped past him.

This was a much faster and safer route to the study as Cassie did not have to pass the sleeping kutches. But the school was not as empty as she expected, and on three occasions Cassie had to hide the glow-bug jar under her skirt. As she tiptoed past the kitchen she spotted Mrs Sandskrit having a late-night sea pasty snack. Calluna was in the practice room going over and over the dance moves with a determined and frightened look on her face and Miss Youngsand Jnr was in the science lab testing sand samples.

Cassie felt calm this time as she carefully picked the lock.

The glow-bug jar made it so much easier to move around the room. Cassie made straight for the window. She placed her light on the floor and used both hands to feel along the window seat for the catch.

The soft clicking and her breathing were the only sounds. Cassie's hands trembled as she reached inside and pulled out the pages.

She took a long, deep breath, and began to read.

Miss Youngsand Jnr has completed her scientific studies and reported to the meeting that the dunes are eroding much faster than was feared, and that the time has come when serious action needs to be taken. Sifting sand and performing dune dances are not enough to keep the erosion in check.

The sand farers are coming back with reports of similar

things happening in all the dunes they have visited across the globe.

We sat in silence for a long time. There was a storm brewing, but Sandrine told the meeting that another visitor was expected. She arrived a few minutes later, apologising for her lateness – she had to put her daughter to bed.

Marina Marramgrass is the finest sand dancer the school has ever produced and the most excellent interpreter of the dune dances. She is the perfect sand sprite for the secret mission.

We all performed the Loyalty Dance:

Travelling, travelling on through our lives
Hoping, daring, dreaming,
Looking out and caring for
Our family, friends and the dunes in dangerous times.

After the cups of sage tea had been served Sandrine said there was only one item to be discussed and that no one must hear of it outside this room. Sandrine did not even want her ministers and advisors to know of it in case it caused trouble and discord. She said that the sand dancers were her truest and most loyal subjects. She asked that Marina undertake a secret journey to visit all the dunes in the main continents to see how they were coping with the possible dune destruction and to discover which of their dances were the strongest ones to make the dunes sing and to keep them healthy. If a talented sand dancer could put

together all the sequences to create one powerful dune dance,
she reasoned it might halt the destruction.

Marina agreed immediately, but expressed concerns about
the length of time the mission would take. Sandrine assured
her that she would be able to come back soon. Bad weather
was expected in the next few days, so she must leave with the
sand farers immediately.

The bad weather came much sooner than expected and, no
sooner had she left, than the Great Sandstorm struck – the most
ferocious and destructive storm in living memory.

Cassie continued to read – all about the futile searches for
Marina, to find out if she had survived, and the death of
her father among many other sand farers. She read about
Sandrine's decision that all the sand sprites' energies had
to go into rebuilding Silica City and the surrounding
dunes – this was why she decided to close down the dance
school until further notice. Sandrine had to face fierce
criticism and possible rebellion, but she held everything
together. Until the time when the dance school reopened,
the existing sand dancers had to keep the memory of the
secret dune dances alive.

Cassie closed the pages and returned them to the
hiding place. Then she locked the study and crept
along the corridor. She took a few steps into the main
school and stopped. She rested her head against the wall.
So the dunes were in danger. Sandrine was fierce for a reason. Her mother's disappearance wasn't about jealousy or

sand sprites bearing grudges. It was so much bigger than that! She felt dizzy. Cassie closed her eyes and took some deep breaths as she slowly made her way back to her kutch.

She saw Miss Youngsand Jnr softly snoozing on a workbench in her lab. Cassie understood now why she was working so late into the night. She was trying to save the dunes. There was no sign of Mrs Sandskrit, only a few traces of crumbs on an empty plate. And there was Calluna, lying on the floor of the practice room sobbing, 'I have to get it right, I am the best, I will be the best.' Cassie's heart went out to her – all the other sand dancers would be in bed by now, and Calluna must be exhausted! She must be very dedicated, but also very worried, to be still practising at this hour.

Cassie moved as quickly as she could away from her. She knew that trying to comfort Calluna would be point-less, as she would hate to be seen showing any sign of weakness, and she would be mean to the sprite who saw it.

As she approached the gatehouse she heard the sound of singing.

'Never upset a sand farer
For his memory is as long as time
If you upset a sand farer
He'll fill your bed with slime – YO!'

Cassie popped her head round the door. Thassalinus and Rubus were sitting together on the floor. A red-faced

Thassalinus was sipping from the flask of mead. He growled at Cassie. 'I hope you are not here to upset a sand farer. You should be tucked up in bed!' He turned to Rubus. 'Do you see what I have to put up with?'

Rubus nodded and said, 'I should fill her bed with slime!'

Cassie pretended to look shocked. 'I only came to warn you. I've just seen Mrs Sandskrit heading this way. I am sure she would not approve of night sprites drinking mollusc mead and singing when they should be on duty.'

Thassalinus was instantly on his feet. 'You're right. Now let's be having you. Move along now!'

Rubus bowed. 'Thank you for telling me your stories.'

Thassalinus bowed back. 'It has been a pleasure talking to you. Sand farers are a tough breed. No matter what you throw at them they always come back!'

'It looked like hard work keeping Thassalinus occupied,' Cassie teased as they walked back along the beach.

'It was really interesting to hear about sand farers and their exploits. You have to train really hard.' Rubus paused. 'It'll take me ages to become one.'

'But what about your sand racing? I thought you wanted to be a champion racer too.' Cassie had never seen Rubus look so serious.

'I do, but I am tired of always pleasing myself and drifting. It would be good to have some great stories to tell when I am old. But I can see by the look on your face that you've found something out, so stop asking me questions and tell me all about it!'

They stopped at the foot of Cassie's balcony so she could tell him everything.

As she finished, Cassie found that there were tears in her eyes. 'Oh Rubus, now I almost wish that I hadn't found out. Knowing that the dunes are in danger makes me feel scared. This information changes everything.'

Rubus hugged her. 'You are very brave, Cassie, and you should be proud of your mother.'

'I am,' Cassie whispered.

'I'm sorry, but I'll have to go now before anyone sees us. But I will come back soon,' Rubus promised.

'Please keep this to yourself . . . until we can figure out what to do next,' Cassie insisted.

It was only when she was alone that Cassie flung herself on the bed and cried and cried until she finally fell asleep.

Chapter Sixteen

*'Time passes, sands shift and
secrets are revealed.'*
The Sands of Time

Cassie woke early the next morning with a fresh breeze blowing through her room. As she washed and tied her braids tightly she felt as if a pebble had been lifted from her stomach. *Her mother left her that night to help save the dunes! She had to go because she was the best dancer, and she would be able to piece all the dune dances together into one powerful piece!*

Then other dizzying thoughts overwhelmed her. *Her mother had never returned, so did that mean that the dunes were still dying? Is that why the dance school had reopened? Were the dunes in such a dreadful state that Sandrine desperately needed more sand dancers?*

She wasn't sure what she was going to do next. She

129

was longing to tell everyone what she had found out, but she couldn't. She could easily be expelled for breaking into Madame Rosa's study. She was going to have to do something, but for the moment it was enough just to know the truth and that there was a reason behind her mother's disappearance – that she had been trying to save the dunes. More than ever Cassie knew that she had to become a great sand dancer and that through dancing she, too, would help save the dunes. Perhaps she could do what her mother had not lived to do. Even if she wasn't the best dancer, she would work hard to be as good as she could be.

That day was a rest day but Cassie had not forgotten her promise to Madame Rosa and she decided to do some extra dance practice.

She raced down the corridor to meet Shell and Lexie.

'How are you two going to spend your day?' Cassie asked as she linked arms with them. 'Only I was hoping you could find some time to help me with some dance practice.'

'It is a rest day so I was intending to do just that,' Shell said. 'But I suppose it would be entertaining to watch you stumble about the place!' She winked at Lexie.

'I was going to go over my Dune Arabesques. Perhaps we could do them together?' Lexie said.

'What do you think you are doing?' A familiar voice stopped them in their tracks.

An angry-looking Calluna was waiting at the foot of the stairs. 'The rules clearly state that students must walk single file down the stairs. You are setting a bad example. You can spend the day cleaning out the stock cupboard.'

She turned and quickly left them.

'That's ridiculous! I've a good mind to go to Madame Rosa,' Shell flared up.

'It won't be so bad if we're together,' Lexie said.

'I suppose I could Dune Bug Jump down the shelves!' Cassie sighed.

'Don't expect me to catch you; I'll be too busy keeping the dust out of my hair!' Shell replied.

The stock cupboard was next to the practice room and it was long and crammed with shelves that were spilling out with objects. It was lit with an old musty gas lamp that gave off a strange green glow.

'This will take days to sort out,' Cassie groaned as they all stood in the doorway.

Calluna had left them some thick overalls to wear and some long brushes and pieces of sponge cloths. They turned and looked at each other.

'Don't we look stylish?' Shell struck a pose.

'The green light is *so* flattering,' Cassie joked.

Lexie waggled her long brush and twirled down the cupboard, leaving a cloud of dust after her.

'Let's try to be systematic.' Shell shook her brush. 'We should divide the cupboard into sections and each do a bit. That way we won't choke on the dust.'

Cassie wandered down to the end. 'I'll start here,' she said, standing beside a rickety old stepladder that led up to a shelf full of boxes. She climbed up the ladder and flicked a cloth over the boxes.

'Why do sand sprites never throw anything away?' she called out to her friends.

'Because it might come in useful!' her friends chanted back at her.

As Cassie worked, she thought about the Triple Silica Jump, which she had been practising. She jumped down from the ladder, swung her hips as she closed her eyes and tried to imagine herself performing it.

The first two jumps went fine but she mistimed the third. As she spun round and round her duster got tangled up in the leg of her overall. Feeling dizzy, she reached out with her empty hand to steady herself but all she managed to do was pull out a box. It caught the side of her head and she spun around again as everything in the room began to swirl and dance before her eyes.

It was a smell that brought her to her senses. She inhaled the distinctive scent of roses and sea kelp with a hint of sea breezes. The smell of her mother's favourite perfume. Cassie took a deep breath. Her senses were not wrong. The smell lingered.

'Cassie, are you all right?' a voice asked. Cassie half-opened her eyes. There was the most beautiful dress she had ever seen. A dress that she recognised from the lantern slides. Her mother's dune dancing dress.

Cassie blinked and grabbed hold of an arm. 'Is it you, Mama? Have you come back from your journey? Sandrine had no right to send you away for so long!'

'She's delirious,' another voice said as Cassie felt herself being lifted up.

'Cassie, it's me – Lexie, you've just had a nasty fall. I found this dress in a basket. I couldn't resist putting it on.' Then she gasped. 'Oh Cassie, is this your mother's dress? I'm so sorry. I'll take it off right away.'

'You're going to have a bump on your head,' Shell said, peering at Cassie. 'But there's no blood.'

'Shall I go and get help?' Lexie asked.

Shell and Cassie both said, 'No!'

'It was just the shock of seeing that dress.' Cassie reached out and grabbed some of the fabric and sniffed it.

'You said something about Sandrine . . .' Shell said as she helped Cassie stand up.

'Did I?'

'You mumbled something about Sandrine having no right to send your mother away for so long. What did you mean?' Shell looked serious. 'Please, Cassie, I need to know.'

'Leave her be, Shell. She was probably talking nonsense,' said Lexie as she changed back into her overalls.

'What I said was the truth,' Cassie said softly. 'We said that we wouldn't talk about our pasts, but I have discovered that Sandrine sent my mother on a secret mission to help save the dunes.'

Words came flooding out of Cassie as she told them about the reason why she wanted to be at Sandringham and then about the two secret visits to the study. Lexie and Shell listened with awestruck faces.

'When I read the missing pages I found out that my mother had been sent on a mission to visit all the dunes and learn the secret dune dances from around the world. I'd started to blame Sandrine, but reading those pages made me realise that Sandrine had no choice. She was faced with an appalling decision, and has always felt responsible for my mother's disappearance.'

'Then your mother got caught in the Great Sandstorm. Oh Cassie, I'm so sorry.' Tears welled up in Lexie's eyes.

'You have to promise me that you will not tell anyone about this,' Cassie insisted.

Shell's voice quivered. 'We will keep your secret, Cassie.'

'Of course we will,' Lexie agreed.

'That clears up a lot of things,' Shell said, wiping away a tear.

'What do you mean?' Lexie asked as she handed her a handkerchief.

Shell blew her nose. 'Just about how things are at the palace. Why Sandrine can be so moody sometimes, and the way that she treats Anagallis.'

'You mean that she spoils her and lets her do exactly what she likes,' Lexie said, 'whilst the rest of us have to struggle along the best we can.'

'You don't understand what it is like for Anagallis,' replied Shell. 'When you are given everything you want it can feel like you aren't really loved at all. It's easy just to give things. Sometimes saying no to a demand is a sign of caring.'

After a moment's silence, Lexie stood up and said in a mock solemn voice, 'From now on this place shall be known as the Secrets Cupboard!'

They all linked arms. 'The Secrets Cupboard!' they chanted together.

Shell helped Cassie tidy up the spilled boxes. 'I knew you were hiding something from us!' she said. 'You've been so distracted lately. Lexie thought that perhaps you had a crush on Rubus.'

'I did not say that! *You* said it!' Lexie gasped.

'Shell, you are impossible!' Cassie grinned.

Lexie held up Marina's dress. 'A prima dune dancer's dress! I can't believe I've been wearing it! It is beyond beautiful. Look at these tiny seed pearls and shells stitched together on the bodice, and the skirt is so light.'

'You're gushing again,' Shell warned.

'I just can't help myself.' Lexie stroked the dress.

She helped Cassie fold the dress carefully and put it back in the basket.

'Just before we go, and as we are in the Secrets Cupboard, there is something I'd really like to tell you . . .' began Shell.

Just then, the door creaked open and Ella and a group

135

of the younger sand dancers crept in. 'We've come to help you out,' Ella informed them.

'My news will keep for another time,' Shell said quietly.

'That's really kind of you,' Lexie smiled at the little sand dancers.

When Calluna came to check later on she was surprised at how much they had achieved.

'Just a bit of teamwork and a lot of belief and trust in each other,' Shell told her.

Chapter Seventeen

'When a lot of sand has passed through the timer,
it is easier to see the truth through it.'
The Sands of Time

Finally the night of the Harvest Moon Festival arrived. As the sun began to set, Silica Square began to fill up. A crowd was gathering around the platform that had been built for the dancers to perform on.

Everyone was talking about the dancing.

'Of course they won't be as good as they were in my day,' an elderly sand sprite insisted.

'I've heard they're even better than before, which is amazing considering there are only twenty-five sand dancers at the school,' said another sprite. 'My daughter Alexsandra is one of the eight dancers that have been picked to dance today. I was one of the last sand dancers to perform at the Harvest Moon Festival.'

'And my daughter is Calluna – the senior sand dancer. She had better not let me down,' a severe-looking sand sprite sniffed.

'I'm sure she will do her best,' Lexie's mother, Viola Seacouch, said in a gentle voice.

'Only perfection is good enough. Anything less is disgraceful and will not be tolerated!' Calluna's mother snapped.

Cassie, who had overheard this exchange, felt sorry for Calluna. She must be constantly worried that she was not living up to her mother's high expectations. Was this where her mean-spiritedness came from?

'I'm just glad to see some dancing again at the Harvest Moon Festival,' another sprite added.

Cassie wondered if Euphorbia would be able to get the time off from the sand factory to come to the festivities. At least she would be pleased that Cassie wasn't dancing.

All conversation stopped as a group of silver dune bugs sped into the square. The occupants jumped off and began to clear the way for the large silver bug that was carrying Sandrine.

As fast as quicksilver, a canopy was set up opposite the platform and, after a lot of fussing and handing round of cool drinks, Sandrine took her place on a throne under the canopy. She was wearing a long shimmering cloak and her white braids were piled on top of her head. She looked impressive as she nodded at the crowd.

Then the dune bug carrying the Harvest Moon

dancers from the dance school lumbered into the square. Everyone stopped to look at the sand dancers, and as they walked towards the stage, there was a spontaneous cheer. Madame Rosa and Mrs Sandskrit began to direct them to unpack their things.

A familiar voice beside Cassie said, 'Hope they can dance as beautifully as they look.'

'Rubus, you are wearing a shirt!' Cassie was pleased to see her friend, but shocked. She had never seen him like this before.

'Wouldn't be seen in Silica Square without one,' Rubus said. 'Might make the delicate sand dancers faint!' He elbowed her in the ribs. 'Besides, Euphorbia is here and she would give me such a telling-off.'

'Where is she?' Cassie felt very pleased that her aunt had come.

'She's with Lena Sealovage. They travelled down together from Mite Cove.'

There was no more time for talking as the crowd hushed around them. Sandrine was standing on the stage and began to address the crowd.

'The Harvest Moon Festival has always been a special occasion for sand sprites. It is a time to meet up, to relax and enjoy each other's company. As you know, the famous Sandringham Dance School has reopened and today we will see some of the finest dancers perform.'

There was a big cheer from the crowd. As Sandrine walked slowly off the stage the curtains were pulled back and the eight dancers stood in their positions. Nothing moved, apart from their costumes in the light breeze.

Cassie felt a huge pang of disappointment that she wasn't up there. She watched Lexie, Shell and Ella and felt pleased for them. She wanted them to dance their best and show everyone how good they were.

The sand dancers performed their first set of exercises perfectly and everyone cheered. Mrs Sandskrit came on stage and announced, 'After that demonstration of skills we will now attempt a short dance piece.'

It was time for the interpretative dancing display.

Cassie watched. It was beautiful as the dancers moved around the stage. They looked so free and fluid and relaxed, but Cassie knew that each step had been perfectly choreographed and timed.

They were just completing the sand gliding and moving from some jumps into arabesques when Calluna made a miscalculation with her feet and stumbled. It was only a slight fault and few sprites would have noticed as she quickly righted herself and carried on.

'The idiot! I'll box her ears for that!' Calluna's mother hissed from the side of the stage. She pulled an angry face at Calluna, who tried her best to continue but seemed to get worse as she noticed her mother's reaction.

The dance ended, and Madame Rosa and Mrs Sandskrit appeared on stage. They assembled all the dancers, who stepped forward and curtseyed. Everyone clapped and cheered.

Then the crowd fell silent as Sandrine rose slowly from her seat on the platform opposite the stage. Her face was expressionless, but her presence was commanding.

Then she began to speak, and her face relaxed into a smile. 'The dance school has been closed for seven long years but, as I watched that wonderful display, it seemed as if the sands of time had been turned back and that the Great Sandstorm had not blown, bringing with it such destruction and devastation. Let us take a moment to remember all those sand sprites who perished that day.'

Everyone bowed their heads.

'And now it is time to move forward. Seven long years of hard work and rebuilding have restored our beautiful dunes and now we have our sand dancers back!'

Everyone began to cheer and clap as Sandrine nodded and continued. 'I would like to thank Madame Rosa and her staff for all their hard work.'

'Don't forget the sand dancers!' Lexie's mum called out.

'No indeed. These young sand dancers have been a source of pride to me. I must admit that when I was holding the auditions, I was not sure if we had the talent, but these shining sandbeams have proved me wrong.'

Madame Rosa curtseyed. 'I would like to thank you, Sandrine, for repealing Rule 623 and allowing us to, once again, devote our lives to dancing.'

At the far corner of the crowded market there was some jostling and Cassie spotted Thassalinus roughly pushing his way through the crowds. Another sand farer was by his side. He was leaning against Thassalinus and he was gasping for breath.

'Make way, make way,' Thassalinus bellowed.

The crowd stopped grumbling and the wave of disapproval turned into something else as they realised that the sand farer must have returned from a long and dangerous journey. Rubus rushed over and supported his arm. The sand farer nodded his thanks.

The crowd parted like marramgrass in the breeze to allow them to make their way towards Sandrine.

As he approached the Supreme Sand Sprite, the sand farer seemed to draw on his last reserves of energy. He pulled away from his helpers and stood tall and proud before Sandrine.

He bowed low. Then he began to cough and sank to the ground.

'Water,' Sandrine ordered.

Thassalinus handed him a flask. 'Take a drop of mollusc mead. That will put some fire in your belly.'

The sand farer gratefully took a sip.

Thassalinus bowed to Sandrine. 'I found this poor soul this morning wandering around the outskirts of Dreamy Dune. He refused to rest and insisted that he had to speak with you at once. He told me that he could not rest until he had passed on some information. Only then would he be able to return to his home dune.' Thassalinus helped the sand farer to his feet.

'I have some important news,' he informed Sandrine.

Sandrine took control. 'Put him on a silver bug. We will go at once to the palace and hear your news!' She turned to the crowd. 'Continue with the celebrations.'

The crowd sighed with disappointment. It had been seven long years since a sand farer had returned to Silica City, and they were hungry for news.

Chapter Eighteen

'Time and tide cannot go back.
Go forward!'
The Sands of Time

No one moved from the square. Sand sprites huddled in groups whispering about what they had just seen. The sand dancers sat on the stage. Half an hour had passed since Sandrine had swept the sand farer away.

'He must be bringing some really serious news,' Cassie said, as she helped Lexie take off her dancing slippers. 'Are you sure your leg is all right?' She had noticed Lexie wince with pain.

'I hope so. It's just some muscle strain. I pulled something on the last Dune Bug Jump of the dance.'

'You must look after yourself, Lexie. You're always running around after other sprites, taking care of Shell and Ella. Don't neglect your own health,' Cassie warned.

Lexie smiled. 'You're all my friends. Ella is so young, and Shell – well, she's naturally bossy. Where is she?'

'She hopped into Sandrine's silver bug,' Cassie replied.

Lexie laughed. 'Shell can talk herself into anywhere – she is a natural leader.'

A thought landed with a splash in Cassie's head, like a pebble in the middle of a rockpool, as memories of Shell flickered in her brain – on the silver dune bug overloaded with luggage, helping herself to food, expecting things to be done for her . . .

Cassie felt a sharp tap on her shoulder. When she turned round she saw that it was Shell – only she was wearing a silver cloak like the one Sandrine wore.

'Sandrine wants to see you,' she whispered as she began to lead Cassie by the arm towards a silver bug.

Cassie looked carefully at Shell and then dropped her head saying, 'As you wish . . .' She started to follow Shell. Then she stopped and finished, '. . . Anagallis?'

Shell stopped. 'There's no time for asking questions.'

Lexie screamed. 'I do not believe this! I think I really am going to faint now.'

Cassie and Shell steadied her.

'That is why you did not want to talk about the past!' Cassie said. 'You are Anagallis. I'm sorry, Shell. I've said so many awful things about Sandrine, without even knowing her. I know now that she wasn't being spiteful and that I was wrong to blame her for my mother going away.'

Lexie blushed. 'When I think of all the nasty things

we've said about Anagallis too . . .'

'I said a few things about her myself,' Shell laughed.

Cassie nodded. 'I recall something about her being as fat as a barrel and not being interested in dancing.'

'I knew that I would be treated differently if everyone knew who I was. I wanted a chance to prove myself. As soon as people know you are Sandrine's daughter, everything changes,' Shell explained.

Cassie nodded. After all, she had intended to keep the fact that she was a Marramgrass a secret until Rubus had made that impossible. Then she smiled to herself, thinking about how Calluna would react if she knew she was being so mean and spiteful to the Supreme Sand Sprite's only daughter.

'We'll talk about this later, but you really do have to come to Sandrine now.' Shell took Cassie's arm.

From out of nowhere Euphorbia and Rubus appeared beside her.

'She's going nowhere without me,' Euphorbia warned.

Rubus stood by Cassie. 'Me too.'

'Sandrine has only asked to see Cassie,' said Shell.

Euphorbia stomped her stick down hard dangerously close to Shell's toes. 'Listen to me, young lady, and don't think I have forgotten for one minute the trick you played on me at the auditions. You have no right to tell me —'

Cassie interrupted. 'Aunt, let me introduce you to Anagallis, daughter of —'

'I know who Anagallis is,' Euphorbia cut in, then she

turned pale. 'Oh I see – *you* are Anagallis.' She curtseyed.

Rubus laughed. 'Nice trick to play on us. Of course I guessed it ages ago. Ouch!'

Cassie had kicked him. 'You did not.'

Shell sighed impatiently. 'We're late already. Come along if you must.'

They all crammed onto the tiny bug. Groups of sand sprites stood around staring at them.

'Haven't you got sand to be shifting?' Euphorbia waggled her stick at them as they sped past.

At the palace they were shown into a small chamber where Sandrine was lying on a couch sipping a cup of sage tea. Her face was pale but her eyes glowed. She stood up when they came in.

Shell stepped forward. 'Here's Cassie.'

Sandrine put her teacup down and looked at Cassie. 'I remember you from the auditions. You had that fierce Marramgrass look of determination in your eyes.'

Euphorbia curtseyed and added, 'A fine quality for a sand dancer to have.'

'Indeed.' Sandrine smiled. 'Good to see you again, Euphorbia Marramgrass. I have had many good reports about your excellent work at Mite Cove. Your dedication has helped keep the sand clean and pure.'

Euphorbia gave a curtsey of appreciation.

Sandrine's voice turned more serious. 'I have some news . . . about Marina.'

Cassie let out an involuntary gasp.

'Cassandra. I have brought you here to tell you that the sand farer has reported a possible sighting of Marina. He is certain that he glimpsed Marina through his telescope. She was dancing in a dune many continents from here. She seemed well and in good spirits. The sighting was a few months ago but it appears to be a good lead. The sand farer knew your mother and father well. He could not reach the dune safely as it was a particularly inaccessible one, so decided to make his way back here as swiftly as he could. I do not want to say too much at this point, but I am sending a large sand galleon to investigate at first light. There is no time to be lost.'

Shell hugged Cassie. 'Isn't it wonderful news! It seems like your mother is alive.'

Euphorbia collapsed into a nearby chair. 'I had almost given up . . .'

Cassie could hardly concentrate as Sandrine talked to her about Marina, explaining what had happened on the night of the Great Sandstorm. Sandrine also explained how dedicated Marina was, and how painful it had been for her to leave her daughter behind. Finally she said, 'If Marina is alive and yet has not come back to us, then there will be a good reason for this – we need to go to her and find out what this reason is.'

When Sandrine had finished speaking, Rubus stepped forward, his face suddenly serious. 'Sandrine, I would like to ask your permission to go on the journey.'

Sandrine looked at him. 'You are very young.'

'I am a good navigator. I have been racing my own small sand surfers for years. It would give me some direction, a chance to prove myself. I would like to become a sand farer.'

'It will be a long and dangerous journey.' Sandrine's expression was stern.

'I can pull my weight,' Rubus replied. 'If the wind is in the right direction, I can pull ten times my weight.'

'Very well, Rubus,' said Sandrine after a long pause. 'You have my permission to join the expedition.'

'Then I want to go along as well.' Cassie pushed herself forward.

'I forbid it,' Euphorbia said quickly.

'It is a brave offer.' Sandrine smiled. 'But your task is to remain at Sandringham. Anagallis will also be staying, even though I had agreed that she could stay only for a term. It seems that she really does have some aptitude for dancing. You all need to perfect your dancing, for I have a feeling that we are going to need our sand dancers more than ever.'

Chapter Nineteen

'Draw a line in the sand
and then go out and have fun.'
The Sands of Time

Later that night in the main corridor of Sandringham, Lexie said, 'Are you sure we should be doing this?'

'Shh!' Shell pressed a finger to her lips as they all tip-toed past the main staircase and crept into the kitchen.

Cassie cut off some slices of laver bread and slipped them in her pocket.

Lexie looked worried. 'We're not allowed out at night.'

'That's the whole point,' Shell hissed, 'of having a secret moonlight picnic.'

'Besides, we've arranged to meet Rubus. Don't forget it is his last night before he leaves, and I challenged him to a sand boarding race,' Cassie added as she popped a crumb into her mouth.

'Come on.' Shell waved them out of the door, and when they were clear of the dance school they scooted down the side of the sand dune towards the beach. The more speed they picked up the more they flung out their arms and screamed.

'Wheee! This is fun!' Lexie yelled.

'I'm so glad that Sandrine is letting you stay at the school, Anagallis,' said Cassie as they unpacked their picnic.

'Shell! Please call me Shell! At Sandringham I am just another sand dancer,' she said.

Cassie smiled. 'All right,' she replied. 'This is such a beautiful place.' She sighed as she leaned back on the edge of the dune and looked up at the night sky.

'So beautiful and so fragile, it's hard to believe it could all disappear,' Shell whispered.

'Sand is always shifting and life is changing. That's a Rule, isn't it?' Lexie asked.

'But what if we couldn't look after the dunes any more?' Shell lay back in the sand. 'Sometimes there is talk at the palace about more sandstorms that could be even stronger than the Great Sandstorm, or of giant waves that could appear out of nowhere and wash all the dunes away.'

Cassie looked at her friend. She had never seen her look so serious before. Cassie squeezed her arm. 'We are dancing again. Next term we will start to learn the steps of some of the secret dune dances.'

'That will be so exciting!' Lexie gushed. 'I can hardly believe that we're going to be a part of it all!'

'I'm going for a moonlight stroll. The moon makes everything look different.' Shell stood up.

'I'll join you.' Lexie followed.

'Only if you stop gushing!' Shell joked.

'Oh yes, Your Majesty,' Lexie giggled, mock curtseying.

'Supreme Sand Sprite in-waiting to you,' Shell laughed.

'I'll wait here for Rubus.' Cassie lay back on the sand.

So much had happened to her in the past weeks. She had left Mite Cove and learned to love dancing. She had discovered that her mother had left her because by doing so she was doing her best for the dunes. And she had discovered that her mother might be alive. She was so excited she felt as if she was going to explode into trillions of grains of pure happiness.

A lump of damp sand landed in her lap.

'Rubus!'

'Hope you've saved me some of the picnic.' He sat down beside her.

She flicked the sand off. 'You are late.'

'I had a few things to organise,' he explained.

'Are you sure you want to go on this journey? It might be dangerous.'

Rubus's eyes flashed. 'I hope so!'

'Please be careful.' Cassie suddenly felt afraid for her friend.

'Course I will. I have to come back and torment you, don't I?'

'It will be a relief not to be embarrassed in public in the meanwhile.' Cassie tried to smile but she suddenly found herself close to tears and, without thinking, reached out and hugged Rubus.

He hugged her back. 'I will be careful, Cassie. I won't take any unnecessary risks.'

'Send me a message as soon as you find my mother,' Cassie said. 'And when you do find her, tell her I haven't forgotten her. Tell her I'm dancing and that I am trying to become one of the finest sand dancers.'

She quickly wiped away a tear.

Rubus bowed and kissed her hand. 'I will, Cassie.' He looked up to see Shell and Lexie who had just returned. 'And now, for one last time, let's race!'

Rubus waved at Lexie. 'I've brought my sand board and Cassie can lend you hers, so prepare to be beaten! I haven't forgotten about that promise you made to tan my hide!'

'I'll try anything once,' Shell said and tucked her flowing skirts into her knickers.

The others giggled as they set off and they took turns at racing Rubus down the edge of the dune.

Cassie laughed as she launched herself down the dune for what seemed like the hundredth time. At first they raced along the beach neck and neck. Sometimes Rubus pulled into the lead and sometimes Cassie did.

'I'm going to beat you this time,' Cassie yelled to Rubus as her friends cheered her on.

'Consider yourself beaten,' she declared triumphantly as she crossed the seaweed finish line. 'We have tanned your hide.' Cassie looked round at her friends. 'We are all going to be fine,' she told them. And, gripping each other's arms and smiling widely, they all sang:

'Day and night,
Loyal and true
I will always believe the best of you
I'll share my time
I'll stick like glue
Never a flicker of doubt for you
I'll watch your back
I'll sift your sand
If you fall I'll take your hand
No question
No need for answers
With your friendship I'll take a chance
Do what's fun
Do what's right
Because
You're a true friend of this sand sprite.'

I sneaked out of the caravan late one moonlit night and went for a walk on the sands. I saw four tiny little creatures skateboarding down a sand dune. They were laughing and screaming. One of them had her skirt tucked into her knickers. My mum says I must have been dreaming, but I know I wasn't. And so do you!

Betsy Root, aged 12, 2009

Explore the dunes,
the dance school,
and lots more at:

www.thesanddancers.com